Easter Sunday

A novel by

Thomas Hollyday

Published by Solar Sipper Publishing, Division of Happy Bird Corporation, PO Box 86, Weston, MA 02493

~ v2 ~

Print ISBN number 978-1-5150182-9-2

Kindle ASIN: B011C9O3IM

"He saw the face of his son and was bewildered"

- From an early German Christian poem
about Joseph the father of Jesus

Chapter One

It was the day before Easter Sunday.

Bobby looked up from his grandfather's letter. He folded the pages and stared angrily at his father, Hank Green, who was beside him. Since opening this long awaited letter, to be read only on his twelfth birthday, the boy's face had changed from anticipation to disappointment. Bobby took another moment to examine a pointed black metal object attached to the last page. It looked like a small black crucifix. Bobby inserted all back in the envelope.

Hank watched with growing concern as Bobby crushed the letter into the pocket of his jeans. A white corner showed from under his oversize black and orange Brooks Robinson baseball shirt.

The boy, thin and tall from baseball practice, turned to leave. He said slowly to himself, "Not never." "Not never," he repeated with emphasis, scuffing the wood floor of his father's store. He strode outside, knocking over one of the carefully arranged pots of Hank's prized white daffodils. Bobby stopped for a moment, bent down and set the pot back on its shelf.

The boy reached the street outside and stood silhouetted in the hazy sunlight. Dark clouds grew in the southern sky. His friends waited on their bicycles. Cathy Allingham, another twelve-year-old, rangy and tall, yelled in her tough voice, "Hey, what did the letter say? Did your grandfather leave you some money for your birthday? Are you going to get a boat?"

Bobby pedaled off without answering her and she followed, barely keeping up. The other friend, Richard Solomon, a chunky black boy, rushed after his friends, puffing weakly, "Wait up, you guys, wait up."

Hank, still surprised, ran to the door, calling down the tree-lined street. The children pedaled more than a hundred yards away. He called again, "Bobby, we have to talk about this. Come back!"

The boy either didn't hear or didn't intend to stop.

Hank looked after him.

Whatever my father wrote was wrong. Twelve is too young to spring something distasteful on a kid.

Not more than two hours later, the fire alarm went off.

During Hank's childhood, always when he heard that siren, he thought that his father, who had been Chief of the Volunteer Firemen, would be in danger. After Bobby's birth, however, Hank changed his focus. He began to worry that instead it was Bobby who might be in danger.

Hank listened as two rescue trucks roared out of town. He shook his head again about Bobby's disappointment and anger at the letter. A few minutes later, he sat at his desk planning his annual stroll through town. He had done this for years. He had given daffodils to the town parks and took his walk to photograph them in the spring when they bloomed. He was a gardener, like his father had been, an average height, handsome man approaching middle age, still with all his hair and possessing a strong body kept tough by his outdoor work. He thought about the past years, his former wife, his young son, Bobby, his father and mother now gone, his friends, and the steady life he had found here. A song ran through his mind about the green grass of home, an old Vietnam song.

The phone rang and the town fire alarm went off again, the two echoing against each other.

The police dispatcher was on the line. "It's your son, Mr. Green. There's been an accident at the Wilderness."

Hank's stomach lurched. All his concerns came back, the alarm ringing a tardy reminder that he should have gone after Bobby when his son left in such a distraught mood. He glanced at the wall clock as he ran through the store. Seven o'clock. It would soon be dark at the Wilderness, almost night. He grimaced as he thought of the letter again, that somehow it might have caused Bobby's accident, made him careless, and affected his judgment.

Outside it had begun to rain. In a few moments Hank was on the way, leaning over the steering wheel of his old white delivery truck. Its headlights shone weak in the road shadows, the engine racing as fast as it could.

The Wilderness, a large swampland, was a few miles out of town. He anxiously scanned the road. Off to his right he finally saw what he had been searching for. The headlights flashed on the new Maryland State Road sign Great Wilderness Swamp National Wildlife Refuge. Behind it were the remaining graffiti covered stones of the former monument naming the wetland for a Confederate victory in Virginia in 1864.

Hank turned, the vehicle leaning, almost on two wheels, as it entered the sandy, rain-puddled road. Between the overgrown hedgerows the vines and bushes scratched the truck metal. The cinder-block ranger station loomed on his left. Beyond the building was a large stand of towering loblolly pines leading to the swamp and the boat landing.

Beside the road he saw the line of trees of various ages that his family had donated over the years to the swampland property. Hank's father had planted them with him. Then, when Bobby was a child, Bobby had helped to place the trees. Behind them, far off, were the porch lights of Pete Smithfield's farmhouse. He rounded another turn and ahead were the blinkers of fire trucks and rescue vehicles scattered along the sodden edge of Pete's lower field.

Hank pushed the old nursery truck harder and faster across the ruts, springs bumping, metal creaking, black earth spattering the white sides of the truck. Some of the plants stored in the back ready for delivery tomorrow tipped to the steel-ribbed floor. The tied stalks rolled back and forth with the pitching of the truck, earth spraying from the roots.

Hank reached the landing and slid to a stop. He tore out of the front seat, leaving the headlights beaming ahead and the door open. He shook his head in frustration as he tried to run forward, slowed by the wet gusting wind. His clothes were soaked as he splashed across the wet ruts toward the small group of men by the dock.

The glare from a burst of lightning only a few miles away lit the taut exhausted faces of the men.

"Hank," shouted Sammy, Chief of the River Sunday Volunteer Fire Department, his face wrinkled from years of working in the hot Maryland sun, his fire coat glistening from the rain. Hank saw Bobby's red and white bike leaning against the fence by the pier.

As if he were comforting Bobby, Hank stopped, and while the others waited, gently took a nearby tarpaulin to place over the wet metal frame of the bike. Then he turned, wiped his eyes, and walked quickly with Sammy toward a workboat thumping against the pilings as the open swamp water billowed in, driven by the gusts. Beyond the pier, the marsh stretched hundreds of yards through tall reeds. Swamp grass higher than a man circled treacherous tiny floating islands of mud. The swamp covered a vast area, over a hundred square miles of wetland reaching to the Chesapeake Bay. These reeds hid the channels. The water appeared formidable especially when it was rough with the passing gusts, but actually the swamp was not deep. Hank knew the real danger was in the soft bottom. The federal wildlife scientists had taken core samples and found it mysteriously went down forty or more feet with no hard bottom discovered. They said that if a person got caught he might be sucked under and never found.

Sammy said, leaning over the boat, "The two kids that were with Bobby, they're up to Pete's house, out of the wind."

"Where is Bobby?" Hank asked, his words quick, urgent.

"He's down in a cave under the old burial mound," said Sammy.

Sammy pressed the starter. The outboard turned over and misfired, a large cloud of white smoke blowing over the two men. He inspected the gasoline line and as he worked, he swore. Sammy was a gaunt man, his voice hoarse from cigarettes.

"There," he said. The engine roared spray out from the stern. Sammy added, over the noise of the engine, "I left a message for your ex-wife, too."

"Try Will Allingham," said Hank, not shaking as much, more in control of himself.

"They're all up at her annual Easter Party."

"I guess I don't understand about that anymore," said Hank.

"Wish your father was still alive," yelled Sammy. "We'll sure miss him in the crew today."

Hank nodded. All the firemen remembered his father. He had been the one they depended on in emergencies. Sammy had taken over the Department after Hank's father died.

The engine cavitated, losing its grip, then screamed with high-speed revolutions. Its propeller caught in the weed and then released, the burned oil smell of the exhaust drifting by. The rain eased to a weak drizzle as they headed out.

"Dig him out is all I know," said Sammy. "The kids said your boy mentioned some air blowing into his face just before the cave fell in. He mighta crawled back into a muskrat den, with air vents back under the ground."

"Maybe," said Hank.

"Don't know," answered Sammy, steering into another large swell.

It was black night. As they went out from the dock Hank saw Sammy's mouth swearing but the squall worked up, with some harder rain in patches, and the words were blasted into the wind. Sammy moved his free arm toward a larger distant island, a far row of trees, which were little more than shadows. The wind quieted for a moment and Hank could hear him.

"Soft," said Sammy.

"Soft," repeated Hank, as if he didn't believe all this was happening.

"Bad this spring," said Sammy.

"Might get Mudman to help," said Hank, speaking of his closest friend, Henry Parks, a man who had been through high school then Vietnam with him. Mudman had taken over his family's well drilling business and was an expert on working in wet soil.

"Can't depend on him." Sammy shook his head, fighting the tiller against the current. He was referring to the fact that Mudman was usually drunk. The bow of the boat lifted then smashed down on another swell.

"Bobby was just at the store a little while ago," said Hank.

Sammy answered, "You don't expect kids to watch the weather."

The lights of the rescue party grew brighter as they approached. The beam reflections shattered as the rain pelted the swamp surface. The boat turned and twisted while Sammy wrestled to keep headway in the shallow and imperfect channel. Hank, in turn, leaned over the bow watching for sudden snags of broken tree limbs sticking up, sharp spears that would instantly put a hole in the thin metal hull.

"You're still in good water," shouted Hank.

The burial mound was on an island hidden again behind high reeds. The boat turned around another curve in the channel. The spray hit Hank in the face and as soon as he wiped the drips away, more flooded him with its salty taste and swamp smell.

They passed another stand of reeds and the way opened to the island. He could see lights again. He could also hear chainsaws. This was a true island, although too small to have a name on the maps of the Chesapeake Bay. Still, it was a landmass, not like the plots of grass that floated throughout the swamp and often sank as they were stepped on. This land was different in that it was firm and did not move or float. There had been more land to the island when Hank was a child. Over the years, marsh had gradually invaded the drier land. Surviving on what was left were the same tall loblolly pines, stretched in a line like warriors on guard with the irregular needled branches their weapons. The trees were bending hard against the gusts. Along the shoreline of the island were the dozens of holes, usually only a few inches in diameter, where the muskrats had their tunnels.

In the center of the island was the burial mound, the only property still owned by Jimmy Swift's tribe. The place was sacred, dedicated to ancient chiefs of the tribe, those who had fought bravely in tribal wars over the surrounding land. Jimmy Swift was the last of the Nanticokes worshipping the swamp island. The mound was covered with marsh grass and small bushes and flanked by pines. It was about two hundred feet long and more across, at least a thousand feet around, rising fifteen feet or more above the water level and ten feet over the island. Around it the rest of the island was a chaos of inlets and tiny hills and gullies, reeds and trees. The whole of the dry land measured about four hundred yards across and more than a thousand yards in circumference, so that the mound was much smaller. A line of men in fire coats filled sandbags on one of the dry spots beside the sacred hill.

The boat sliced into the beach and stopped, its bow a good foot into the crush of reeds at the shore. Hank stood up quickly and, jumping out of the craft, pulled the bow further up while Sammy shut down the engine.

"We're putting up bags as much as we can, Hank," he said.

The men were constructing a barrier to keep the mound dry. Small work lights barely illuminating the area were around the mound. Other men were cutting back what remained of a large fallen pine. Sammy pointed to where they had already started digging a trench into the end of the mound and laying sandbags to keep back the tide.

"That's where he is, somewhere down in there," he said.

Hank ran toward the lights and past the line of firemen. As he moved ahead, his body bent against the gusting wind, he saw Pete, some called him Old Pete, standing on top of a wall of sandbags. Like the patriarch Moses, Pete was directing the barrier construction. He was a tall, distinctive black man with white hair and a grizzled beard.

Hank climbed up through the slippery earth to stand next to Pete. The large man put his big hand on Hank's shoulder, his voice soft with a slight drawl. "Hank, Sammy'll get him out."

Close by the edge of the mound the pines were swaying with the winds. Pete pointed at the large tree that had been cut away from the mound. "That was the pine sealed Bobby off when it come down. Figure it forced him further into the mound."

Bob Johnny, the Ranger, a young man with a short beard, stepped forward from the darkness, a dripping shovel in his right hand. His face was shrouded by a yellow plastic windbreaker, and, when he spoke to Hank, he sounded only a little older than Bobby, "It's like a pile of jelly; we dig and it falls right back in."

"I've seen it like this before," said Pete. "Top of the mound sinks right in under you."

Bob Johnny went on, "He could be far inside, a hundred feet."

Hank felt the ooze under his shoes. Sammy had come up from the boat and announced, "Baltimore weather says storm's main winds are still south, moving up from Norfolk. Airport's shut down."

Hank climbed up the sodden embankment. Bob Johnny was pacing back and forth and said, "We could put a hundred men out here digging for ten hours and we'd be lucky to clear out a quarter of this mound."

Sammy said, "If we had time, we'd build a cofferdam, then excavate. Best we can do is filling sandbags. There's some instruments might pick his up body heat but can't get them either. Nothing we can get over from Baltimore in this weather."

"Jimmy was here first thing. Jimmy always hears about things, don't know how," said Pete. "He told me to do what we have to do to get Bobby out. He says there's too many dead already in that mound."

"That old man is not the only person who says what about the mound," said Bob Johnny.

"Yeah, but his people are the owners and you Park Rangers aren't, Bob Johnny," said Pete. "What do you want to do? Just walk away?"

"Hank, I marked where we think the entrance was." Pete pointed to a stick planted in the side of the hill. "Jimmy said he'd be back when we need him, whatever that means."

"I want to see for myself. Just let me see," Hank said, his voice breaking. He clambered in front of the team digging the trench and grabbed handfuls of the wet earth in a frenzy of trying to get at his son.

Pete called to him, "You can't do it by yourself."

Hank moved slowly back, his clothes covered with the slippery black mire. He remembered the baby boy in his arms. He was a younger man again carefully holding the new child. He held the bottle to the boy's lips and watched as the smile came over the little face. There was a trust in those little eyes that the father would not let the child fall down, would not let the child get hurt, ever get hurt.

The image faded. He blinked, tears in his eyes.

"If Jimmy Swift isn't concerned, I am," said Bob Johnny, staring at Sammy, his voice beginning to shrill.

Hank stared at him and started to clench his fist as he realized the ranger was more concerned about the destruction of the swamp and his job than the survival of his son.

Pete said, "Don't pay him any attention, Hank." He addressed the park ranger, who was at least a third of his age. "You leave your kid down there if you were in this mess?"

"No," said Bob Johnny, not meeting Hank's eyes.

"Well, then, don't worry about your job," said Pete.

Sammy spoke up. "This is a Goddamn emergency, boy, and Jimmy recognizes that." He spit. "Far as I'm concerned, a swamp like this, it's God's mistake. Reverend Blue says that the Lord did it all in six days; damned if I don't think He took off too early." He spit again, "I never could understand what Jimmy and the birdwatcher people, any of them, want to save the mound for nohow."

Hank grabbed the shovel from Bob Johnny and moved stubbornly forward. He began to dig with the others, as fast as he could, with a special strength, fueled by a father's love, unreasoning and simple.

Garth Brook's song about thunder pounded in his mind as he worked.

Chapter Two

Sammy looked out over the swamp and shook his head. Then he leaned over to Hank and said, "Let the others dig for a while. I need you to come along with me. We got to get Will Allingham's tractor from the other side of the swamp."

The ranger glanced up from his work. "Sammy, you ain't bringing a tractor in here?"

Sammy turned and answered Bob Johnny, "You got an opinion?"

"Nossir, no, I don't." The ranger shook his head and went back to his shoveling.

Hank noticed the trees swaying. "Sure. However you can use me."

"I'd like you to drive the barge on which Will stores his tractor. I'll pull it but I want you to steer it behind me all the way back here," said Sammy.

"It's hard for me to leave Bobby," Hank said.

"You can be more help to him doing this than standing around worrying."

Hank was silent for a few moments and then nodded. He followed Sammy toward the boat.

"What about more of those trees coming down?" he asked.

"Forestry team from over to Denton is due out here soon to cut them away," said Sammy.

Bob Johnny, standing behind them, said loudly, so Sammy would hear, "We got to be careful with tearing up the mound."

Hank turned. "Let's get going."

"Will Allingham don't like anyone running that tractor without him. Maybe we should wait for him," suggested Bob Johnny.

Hank's face reddened with anger. "Bobby'll be dead before all that happens."

Pete approached them. "Will doesn't want anyone bothering his fencing out there in the swamp," he said, holding up some large wire cutters and smiling.

Sammy looked over. "Pete, I think you might enjoy that job."

Pete nodded with a grin.

Hank talked over his shoulder to Pete as he headed out. "We got less than five hours before this storm flood," he said. "Five hours."

Sammy coughed. "Yessir, that storm surge reach to the mound, old Chief Nanticoke or some of them Nanticoke heroes going to float up from their graves and ride right out to the Bay."

Pete, striding fast to keep up, reached out his arm to Hank's shoulder. "Hank, you going to be all right?"

"I don't know." Hank slowed down and turned his head to Pete. "Do you understand?" Hank asked with his eyes wide open. Hank knew that Pete knew him better than most.

"It's going inside the cave bothering you," answered Pete. "Your father was the same way, never would go inside a closed in place."

Hank nodded.

Pete said, "You must be suffering."

Hank looked down. "My kid never asked anything of me and now this."

They reached the boat. Hank, the last to get in, pushed off and as he did, he said, "He's twelve years old today."

"He'll be having his birthday cake up here with all of us in a couple of hours," said Pete, sitting down in the bow.

Sammy looked over. "Bobby was talking about getting some money from his grandfather. Told me last week he wants to use it for a boat for the two of you."

Hank nodded. "The letter, yes."

Pete patted him on the shoulder. "Well, the money will still be there when this is all over."

Hank turned to Pete, his face in pain, "I've got to do what's right for him."

Pete said, his voice low, his eyes kind and sympathetic, "You'll do fine."

Sammy started the engine. Hank watched truck lights arriving on the mainland, standing out against the distant shape of Pete's house.

"That's the tree men," Sammy said. "They had a tough time getting through the bad roads."

Pete aimed his flashlight toward the darkness of the swamp. Brief interludes came between the gusts, when the air would get warmer, almost stifling and full of marsh fog and stink that competed against the men's own sweat. Then the chill came back with the wind noise and splashed up spray, like winter flailing the hope of spring.

As Sammy backed his boat from shore, a rowboat with a small engine was coming in. In it was Cathy Allingham, Will's twelve-year-old daughter from his first marriage, her mother long gone from River

Sunday. In front sat Richard, Bobby's other friend. Hank caught the gunwale of the craft as it slowed and nosed close.

Cathy leaned forward, buried in the blue slicker that Hank recognized as one of Pete's old farm coats. She stuck her free hand tight in a large side pocket. A bit of her brown hair could be seen strutting from under the plastic hood. Her eyes told Hank she was scared.

"Just tell us what happened, Cathy," said Hank, trying to put her at ease.

She spoke quickly, getting all her story out fast, almost yelling, the wind tearing away parts of her words. "We thought it would not rain until later and we wanted to get up to the swamp and look around. We went ahead and took this outboard at the landing. Pete told us plenty of times we could use it if we tied it back up right."

She caught her breath. "Bobby was insisting we visit the burial mound so we stopped there first. Then we were going out to some of the other islands. Richard and I wanted to find the P47 for the reward."

Sammy spat. "Damn him. Allingham's been offering a hundred dollars to anybody finding his aunt's airplane that went down out here in the War," he said. "He's a damn fool for a teacher. Ought to be ashamed getting them all worked up. Nobody's ever going to find it. Not here anyway."

Hank shook his head.

She went on, "When we came up on the bank, I pointed out a cave that had been opened up. I found one thing on the ground. Then Bobby got excited and wanted to go in and look around."

Hank asked, "He wanted to climb into the hole?"

Cathy nodded. "Yessir, he did," she continued. "I told him the mound was real soft, but he went anyway. Richard and I just watched. Then we heard him yelling about fresh air blowing against his face. He went on about the ceiling of the cave was dripping and some dirt was coming loose. I called to him again to come on out right away.

"About then, Richard and me, we heard the tree falling, a big cracking sound, one of the tall ones behind the mound. We managed to jump back. Its trunk hit and pushed the earth down. We heard Bobby screaming. That's when we tried to get the opening cleared but the tree and the branches were all over the place. The ooze was coming up to our knees and we were afraid the mound would cave in. We called but Bobby didn't answer. That's when we decided to go to Pete's for help. That's the truth, Mr. Green."

Pete motioned to her. "Show them what you found."

She reached in her pocket. "This was near the mouth of the cave. I just hope the firemen can get Bobby out." She pulled her right hand out of the large raincoat pocket and held it forward, trembling, like she was making an offering.

"We're going to get him out," Sammy said, his face kinder than his usual roughness, and showing that he sensed her worry.

"Me and Richard are sorry about Bobby," she said.

Richard nodded. "I feel real bad, Mr. Green."

Sammy took the object from Cathy. "It's gray and shaped like a triangle," he said.

Pete glanced over Hank's shoulder. "Might be a religious object left with those buried Nanticoke chiefs." He thought for a moment then said, "No, that's no relic from Jimmy's people. Their stuff was iron and iron doesn't get gray."

Sammy put it in his pocket. "Holy or not, I got somebody to show it to."

Hank pushed the boat away from Cathy's craft. They heard a horn blaring again and again from the mainland. This time, a car's headlights approached the boat dock, their beams rising and falling from the ruts like flailing white swipes.

"That's Will," said Hank.

"That's my father," said Cathy. "He always honks like that."

"We ought to wait," said Sammy, looking at Hank.

"Like hell," said Hank. "Here, you can blame it on me. Say I was running the damn boat and would not turn around." He started to move toward the engine controls.

"Sit down," Sammy said. "I'll do it." He reversed the engine out into the swamp. When he was out about a hundred feet, Sammy shifted to forward, and then with some blue oil smoke, the engine ran up. He headed the boat in a slow arc out into the Wilderness, running along the reeds at the side of the island.

They went by the firemen digging at the cave entrance and the pile of sandbags holding up the walls of the growing trench. Sammy had left his deputy in charge. Above the men Hank could see the branches and heavy trunk of the fallen tree with men still cutting away the branches. Not far behind were the remaining loblollies, waving with the gale.

Then the island was out of sight and the swamp stretched far ahead into the darkness. Pete moved a large flashlight back and forth but the light extended only twenty feet. "We'll pick up the first of Will's fence in about a mile if we can stay on course," he said.

They knew that the closest path to the tractor was through water acreage planted by Will Allingham. The water was stocked with grasses, wild rice and other crops to entice wildfowl into his profitable rental hunting sites. Hank and the others also knew that Will was the type who, given a little bit of power over others around him, liked to exercise that by refusing to cooperate on even the simplest requests. Unfortunately, "One Shot Will" was a person whose meager properties and powers seemed to be in great need by others at significant times. This gave Will a presence above what he deserved. Will himself had been adamant about any of the trappers using his land. He was known for making sure watermen were fined for trespassing by the local judges Will knew. No watermen ever went near his land for fear of the fines.

"Pete, you see any sign of the property yet?" asked Sammy.

"I'll tell you when," said Pete. Then they were quiet, listening to the engine and staring ahead.

As the boat progressed, the flashlight picked up many animals. Some, like deer and squirrels, rested stranded on the small floating tufts of reeds that were being broken loose by the growing swells. Others, the muskrats and raccoons and turtles, some with babies carried above the water by their mouths, were swimming toward higher land. Water snakes, some of them poisonous, curled past the sides of the boat.

"Wildlife sense the storm is coming," said Pete. "They know the surge will bring in all that ocean water and the salt will kill them."

They reached the Allingham fence and the old man raised his hand. "This is the best place to cut the fence," he said.

Heavy overhanging vines obscured Will's fencing. To get to the wire, Hank and Pete had to cut the vines, which were as tough as the steel links. The wood was wet and slippery and they found it difficult to get the blades to grab. Sammy struggled to keep the boat close in to the fence area so that they could work. The current and wind kept moving them into a lopsided position and the craft began taking spray.

Finally Hank said, "I've got steel links in sight. Pete can start cutting." The job was facilitated by the fact that they were between two of the posts and the fence only had to be cut through in the center, in one place. They planned to peel the fence back on both sides toward the poles. Hank went overboard to cut below the surface. The current pushed his arm hard against the fence. The work took several minutes.

"We may have to open the fence more when we see the width of the barge," said Pete.

Sammy said, "I just hope it's still floating. Will didn't lose any money when he got that old barge, that's for sure."

When Hank was back aboard, Pete pushed back one curl of fencing with an oar and Hank held the other. Hank was cold and could feel a throbbing in his shoulder from hitting steel links. The boat squealed as the sharp edges of the cut fence scraped pieces of fiberglass from the sides of Sammy's boat. Then they were through and the fence sections collapsed behind them.

Sammy speeded the outboard as they moved out into the clear. The flashlight did not pick up any brush or small islands on either side of what was a much wider channel.

"We're inside Will's hunting preserve," said Pete.

A marker pole came up on the right side of the boat.

"We'll go a little bit to port," called Pete as he spotted it. "Here's one of his channel markers."

The red metal sign rushed by the starboard side of the boat about six feet away. "No trespassing. By order of William Allingham," Pete read with a chuckle.

The radio sputtered into life. "Chief, come on back."

Sammy reached into his pocket and pulled out the handset. "Sammy here."

"One of my firemen, Charlie, thinks he heard the boy."

Sammy turned up the volume. "Hank, get this," he said. Then he spoke into the radio, saying, "Go ahead."

"Charlie rigged a radio microphone on the end of a pole and put it into some of the muskrat holes. He wanted to see if he could hear Bobby breathing or moving around. All he was getting was animal noises, but he heard a definite thump from one hole."

"A thump?" asked Hank.

Sammy listened as the static drowned out the report. "From what I could get, that's what he said, like something falling," said Sammy. "Only one time. He hasn't heard it again but Charlie's sure it's the boy. He says it was too much noise for any muskrat."

"Does he know how far into the mound it came from?" asked Hank.

"He couldn't tell," said Sammy.

Hank looked ahead for the tractor. Pete saw it first, ahead of them, its metal bobbing with the barge it was on.

Sammy slowed the engine. Coming into sight was a small steel flat-decked craft, rocking and pulling on its lines, its sides not more than two feet above the water. It was anchored and also tied to a wharf. In the center of its deck, lashed down, was the front-end loader tractor. At the stern, built out on a platform, was a large outboard.

"We'll put a line on her bow to tow her, but, Hank, you'll have to get that barge engine running to keep her behind us," said Sammy.

"She's going to be hard to keep from going aground," said Pete.

Hank reached out to catch the barge as they came alongside. His hands found the middle rung of a steel ladder, and as he climbed rust flaked to his touch. The side of the barge was higher than Sammy's boat by a foot and Hank had to grab and throw himself up and off. All the time he was doing this, swells drove the smaller boat against the barge with crashing impacts.

Hank started and idled the barge engine to let it warm up. Then he moved to the front of the square bow area on the barge. "I'm going for a bow line for you," Hank shouted.

"Hook close to the water line," said Pete, standing in the bow as Sammy worked the smaller boat back close to the barge.

Hank grabbed one of the larger lines coiled on the barge deck and bent over the bow, feeling in the darkness for an eyebolt. One hand remained on the edge of the deck to keep his balance and his other reached down into the swamp as the swells kept drenching him. His fingers found purchase and he slipped the end of the tow rope through it. Then he snagged the line and stood up on the deck. Hank threw the coil to Pete who caught it and secured it to a stern cleat in Sammy's boat.

"She'll pull out my transom unless you keep that big engine pushing her forward, Hank," shouted Sammy.

"Let me bring up the line first," yelled Sammy. He put his boat in gear and pulled the towline taut. "Now, let your first anchor go."

As Hank released the anchors holding the barge, the heavy craft slammed hard into the wharf. Pieces of wooden piling and planks crunched and split. Sammy revved his engine and the barge pulled out a few feet into the channel.

"I'm releasing the other anchor," yelled Hank. He dropped the line and ran back to his engine station.

The wharf lines were let go. As Sammy towed the barge into the marsh channel, it slowly tipped to port. Hank steered to counterbalance to the right, but it tipped the other way. He knew what the matter was.

So did Sammy. "She's got a lot of water moving from side to side in her, Hank."

They headed toward the cut in the fence. On the way the craft swung hard into two of Will's hunting blinds which were placed near the channel. Their pine needles and simple construction proved no match for the deadweight of the barge. The small stilt houses built for hiding hunters crumpled. Several dozen decoys linked together with anchor lines tumbled out of storage baskets from the blind into the marsh. They tangled and dragged noisily on the side of the barge for several hundred feet until they pulled underwater and bobbed up loose in the wake.

When they reached the opening in Will's fence, Sammy signaled that he was not going to slow down. Instead his boat pushed back the fence sections. The barge followed and crashed through, pulling down two more post lengths of fence with its momentum and weight.

Hank's shoulders began to ache from holding the steering lever. He prayed that the engine would last. It was coughing already and throwing out smoke. He doubted that Will had spent any money on maintaining it. He looked ahead into the darkness. The island was out in the night far in front of Sammy's boat. Sammy's craft plowed to maintain headway, ugly with its bow high in the air, the weight of the towed barge pulling down its stern. The darkness and rain surrounded the two boats. The weakening flashlight worked back and forth to try to light ahead.

Then, like a tonic, the noises of the island came from ahead of them. Shouts, chainsaws, and generator engines sounded, dim at first, but then loud even over the roaring of the outboard and the rough background of wind gusts and waves. The echoes drifted across the swamp wasteland like wails of swamp animals signaling the coming storm

Chapter Three

Bob Johnny called out from on shore, his voice shrill, "I can hear you out there in the barge but I can't see the rig."

Hank could not see forward. The tractor bulk blocked him.

Pete hollered against the noise of the wind. "You people on the island. Get ready to help us land."

The barge was close to the shoreline of the island. A light went on at the far side of the mound and Hank could spot Charlie getting ready to insert a pole into one of the muskrat holes in the mound face.

"Charlie," he yelled.

Charlie, a short round-faced man about thirty years of age, his yellow coat stained, turned toward Hank. Charlie still held the pole, a small cube of metal and wires attached to the end. He shielded his eyes.

Hank cupped his hands around his mouth and called louder. "Have you found him yet?"

Charlie shook his head and shouted back, "Can't get any sounds except the damn muskrats scurrying around."

Some of the larger lights were aimed out into the swamp making an orb of white on the water. Pete's flashlight worked toward them. Spots of light moved back and forth. The glare now touched the deck of Sammy's boat, and then moved towards the barge.

Sammy pulled his boat to the side. The barge kept forward and hit the flat of the beach. It threw a great wash of marsh water from the impact. The craft stopped only a short distance from the sandbag wall and raised a foot or more of slop in front.

Pete shook his head. "It's not going any further."

"Let's do it," said Sammy.

Hank thought about how his father would have handled this. He could almost see him in his fire coat, his dark hair blowing over to one side in the rain, shouting to him with authority. "My God, boy," he'd have said, "there's just no way we aren't going to get that tractor to work. We got to push and pull some and she's there."

"You'll need the key to that tractor," said Will Allingham. He had finally arrived, his soft, almost whimpering voice sounding strange among the harsh orders echoing along the shoreline. Will was dressed well, a tie correctly knotted at his neck. True to his cautious nature, even though he was now ashore and safe, he still had strapped to his chest a large orange life jacket lettered River Sunday Fire Department.

Will had inherited and ran the small and exclusive private school begun by his father, a school Bobby as well as Richard and Cathy, attended. The school demanded a high tuition, which Melissa paid. From the school, Will undertook his one big civic project, well known to years of graduates. All the school children, from kindergarten to eighth grade helped him each year. Each had a specific job aimed at repairing or repainting the plywood and cardboard full size model of his aunt's P47 warplane. It would be pulled through the town on a lowboy on Heritage Day. Being Will's daughter, Cathy rode on the float in her figure skating costume. Will liked to say the float represented the past, his aunt's long lost plane, as well as the future, his beautiful skating daughter.

Will added, "You guys should have waited for me. How many fences did you tear down?"

Hank called from the barge, "I'll pay for the damage."

Will laughed. "Hank, your rundown garden shop isn't worth enough to pay for my fences."

"I don't need your help searching for my boy," Hank shouted, clenching his fists.

Will stepped back, his grin fading.

Sammy interrupted, "Will, you want to drive your tractor?"

Will said, "You go ahead, Sammy. No need for both of us to get wet."

Pete said, turning to Sammy, "So I guess it's all yours."

Sammy said, sarcastically imitating Will's voice, "Guess so. No need for Will to get wet. " Sammy climbed on the tractor and reached for the controls.

Aside from the small engines for the generators and chain saws, the noise on the island consisted of the shouting of the men and the wind gusts and occasional thunder. The first rumbles of tractor diesel were like a wash of freshness over the dig site. Men heard the cylinders roar and the smoke from the exhaust rise. A cheer went up matching the smile on Sammy's face.

Sammy ordered sandbags moved back to provide room for the tractor. He'd reset these barriers after the machine was in place ashore. The men assembled boards to make ramps and a working platform. When they were all set, Sammy gave the word and throttled up the engine. The tractor inched ahead and then stopped, its wheels spinning on the barge deck.

"All right, let's get some lines on her," ordered Sammy. The men began to pull on a block and tackle as Sammy let go on the tractor clutch. Suddenly a line pulled loose and hit one of the firemen as it flew forward and splashed into the marsh. The tractor lost its traction on the deck and began to slide backward. As Sammy tried to accelerate to compensate, its large rear wheels began to flip the nose of the tractor upward. Sammy shifted to neutral and the tractor idled and stopped sliding.

Pete rushed to the side of the fireman who had been hit by the rope and thrown face down into muck. "Let's get him on the higher ground!"

Two of the firemen had refastened the block and were bringing up the line again.

"One man stay with him," ordered Pete. "He looks to be all right. Come one, we got to keep at this."

"You better get that line taut," yelled Sammy. "She's sliding again." The tractor, gaining traction, inched ahead but slipped to the side.

Will climbed down to work beside Hank and the others. "We almost got her. A bit more." He took off his life preserver, which had become black from the muck being thrown out by the spinning tractor tires. "One more time and we have her in place."

With the last pull, the tractor lurched forward and came down on the ramp. Sammy kept it moving forward well away from the barge. Behind him men came with sandbags, quickly filling in the wall. The barge, without the weight of the tractor, slipped backward. As it reached deep water, the heavy barge engine pulled its stern underwater and the barge, with seams of its rusted steel hull opening, quickly disappeared beneath the waves.

Pete shouted, "Let's get her in action!"

Sammy maneuvered the tractor into the trench. In a few more moments he was cutting his first pass into the mound. A white muskrat skittered by the men, his pink eyes and nose almost glowing against the dark mud. Albino muskrats were rare and the animal drew a murmur. One of the firemen tried to scare the muskrat away with his shovel, missed, and slapped the marsh wetting the men near him.

Pete said, "I must have saved that muskrat a dozen times during last trapping season." Trappers got their permits from Bob Johnny for a short trapping season but were not allowed to trap near the mound.

"Ask Jimmy Swift," said Cathy. "Sachem is likely his grandfather."

Pete smiled at the girl, "I call him Cochise. Maybe it should be Sachem."

Will looked down at his daughter. "Sachem doesn't exist," he said. "I've told you over and over, Cathy. Jimmy is ignorant."

Sammy was running the tractor well into the trench. The diggers climbed out and stood to the side as the blade was lowered. Sammy took his cut into the higher part of the mound and pulled up some of the sandbags as well as earth. The muck splashed down on the men as he backed the tractor on the platform, turned it and dumped the refuse into the swamp outside the sandbag wall. After the tractor was pulled back, Hank and the others went in with shovels to take out the fallen material.

Sammy brought the tractor up again and idled while they hurried to clear the trench for his next cut. "Put some more boards down there. We need something under her tires."

Pete examined the scene. "Sandbags with boards on top ought to do it."

Hank turned to Pete. "The whole mound might come down on Bobby."

"That's the problem with the weight of the tractor," said Pete. "It's a chance we have to take."

"If we don't get him pretty soon, he's a goner anyway," said Bob Johnny.

Sammy gunned the tractor engine and pulled ahead for another bite. The wind gusted flecks of spray up from the marsh surface and they stung Hank's face.

Bob Johnny pointed to the running lights of several boats hovering in the expanse between the island and his ranger station. "More boat lights out there."

Pete shielded his eyes with his right hand as he observed, "Some of them just come around to see."

Bob Johnny shook his head. "No, it's the animal lovers from town, rescuing the wildlife from the storm. They saw that tractor."

"They'll have to understand this is life or death."

"Johnny Swift is out there and old lady Pond, too." Hank knew the ranger was worried local supporters of the muskrat protection program would complain about the destruction of the mound.

Pete chuckled. "Mrs. Robin Pond. Better not let her hear you calling her an old lady." He added, "She might write a letter to that boss of yours in Washington."

"She'll be worried about her muskrats."

"Water rising like this, she's out there picking up stranded animals in her boat."

A new voice came through the tumult. Betty Allingham, Will's sister, called to Hank as she approached along the wet path by the mound. "I saw your daffodils coming up around town, Greenie."

Hank turned. "Bobby is trapped."

"I know. I came to help. Those daffodils are a good omen, Greenie. I'm sure nothing will hurt Bobby."

His father had planted trees. Hank had taken up the call by planting daffodil bulbs in dozens of small gardens for the public to enjoy. He'd done this since childhood earning the nickname "Greenie." He remembered the annual discussions with his father about the daffodils. His father argued Hank should plant trees - that they would last longer, make traditions over many generations. Hank had chosen the shortness of spring as something of his own. He corresponded with daffodil growers all over the country, an expert in his own right.

Betty was a plain appearing woman, the same age as Hank's former wife, but with a warmer personality. Because of that, everyone saw her as beautiful. She stood on the side of the hill smiling at him.

For a moment, Hank almost forgot the horror of his child locked under the mound as he smiled back at her. The worry for his boy, though, was too great. He went back into his work, shoveling the tractor trench more quickly, as if speed might conquer the unknown danger and slow the ebbing slime in front of him.

"I'd like to help," said Betty, coming closer, speaking in an easy going voice. She was clever too, capable of cracking jokes with the guys or sympathizing softly with a hurt swamp animal. The white muskrat scampered by her feet.

Sammy hollered, "You best look out, there, Betty," referring to his ongoing tractor and perhaps, in fun, making a reference to the animal.

"Don't you worry about Cochise," she snapped back. "He and I will get along. Isn't that right, Hank?"

Hank nodded. They had all been kids here in this swamp, kids in the same way as Bobby and Cathy and Richard were. Pet muskrats had been around in those days, too. Betty had always been the best with the animals. His father had liked her, too, because she listened to his stories about flowers. His mother wasn't too impressed with her. She advised Betty was a land-poor aristocrat, meaning she didn't have any money.

"Cochise doesn't mind the storm, do you, Cochise?" The white muskrat sniffed at her black rubber boots. She reached down to pet him.

Cathy had walked along with Betty and said, "Aunt Betty, we're digging up his home, scaring his family."

"The muskrats don't mind. They want to help us find Bobby," Betty said, putting her arm around the girl's shoulder.

Betty had brought coffee. The men gathered around, taking the hot coffee in cups neatly arranged on a tray she held.

She turned to Pete. "You weren't around when I visited the Wilderness a few weeks ago."

"No," he smiled. "Last I heard you were in Africa."

"I came back. I felt like being home again."

Hank knew she had been at the swamp several times during the month, consulting with Bob Johnny on the Federal budget for the wetland. When she came back to Maryland from an African job, she had gone to work for a state wildlife agency in Annapolis. She lived at Will's house.

She smiled at Hank. "I came as soon as I heard it was Bobby." She pointed to the boats with the lights. "Bob Johnny, they are going to be angry as usual. I thought you might need some political help, too."

Bob Johnny nodded. "I'm waiting for 'em to come in here and tell me I'm not doing my job."

Hank had his head down again. He knelt in the trench, loading his shovel by hand to get more material on the blade.

She handed the last coffee to Hank. "I remember you liked black."

"Like 'Nam, Betty," he said, sensing she was there by the smell of her perfume mixed with the fumes of the coffee.

"How is that?" she asked.

"Filling the sandbags reminds me," he said. "He's down there like I was caught in 'Nam, unable to get out. Only I was rescued by a big shining jet airplane that carried me back to the world." He turned his face up at her. "He might not be so lucky."

"You ought to rest for a little while."

"I am all right. I can do this."

"Like your father."

Betty reminded Hank of his mother. The two women had not liked each other, but they shared solid values of nurturing, the ability to love, and respect for others. On the other hand, Betty did not have the one characteristic of his mother that Hank did not admire, the intense religious fervor that looked down on all those who were not as saved as she was. Betty was more inclusive in her group of friends and would have welcomed a Buddhist from Vietnam if Hank had brought home a Vietnamese wife. Hank had no doubt that except for Melissa, Betty had always been his best woman friend, not his lover but his friend. While he had married Melissa, he still treasured his long talks with Betty talking about flowers and trees.

"This isn't your fight," he said.

"Bobby is my friend, too. Everybody loves him as much as you do."

"Maybe more." He kept thinking he should have cared more about Bobby and should have read the letter first. If he had kept it from Bobby, he was sure none of this would have happened. He reached up, took the paper cup, and sipped the coffee. "Thanks."

A fireman called from the shoreline, holding a large carton with wires handing from it. Behind in the boat were long rods, tripods, and a portable generator. "Sammy, where do you want these lights installed?"

Sammy hollered, "Come on, you men. Let's get these floods up so we can see what we are doing."

Hank surveyed the area as he helped to carry the lights. At the beach the boats continued to come and go bringing more supplies and personnel and taking back those who were worn out. The sandbags were double and triple stacked. Yet, it was the trees that continued to worry Hank. The wind and rain made them waver back and forth in the darkness.

In a short time the beams were installed and high up on their skeletal platforms. These lights had been used for many rescues in similar situations and the men felt more comfortable once they were switched on. The generator revved higher. The darkness fled and smiles crossed the men's faces. The lights gave a sense of security, as though the night was under control and the rescue was moving toward success.

On his way back from the final light installation, Hank lifted another sandbag to his shoulder to carry to the trench. His mind roamed to a recurring image of his little son, trapped below, clawing at the earth which constantly fell back upon his young body. The lights, instead of security, gave Hank only more thoughts about Bobby's closed in place, a horror he feared himself, the horror of the spots where the lights did not reach, the darkness.

"God let him see this light soon," Hank thought. In his mind he remembered the plaintive song of Fleetwood Mac's landslides.

Chapter Four

The sandbag wall was approaching waist height along most of the lowest shoreline near the mound. Meanwhile, Bob Johnny grumbled to anyone who would listen that it was slow work. The walls of the excavation were constantly caving back into the cleared area. The workspace was cramped with about twenty people actively digging. The rest waited to spell them on shifts, meanwhile filling and piling the sandbags. The job had been well organized by Sammy. As many were working as could be accommodated and the others, probably fifty more volunteers in heavy raincoats and with assorted rescue gear, were ready to do their part if asked. The chief himself drove the tractor forward and backward, scooping and dumping. Unfortunately, much of what the machine pulled out simply oozed back around the sandbags.

The wind blew ripples in the plastic of Pete's thin slicker. As he pulled it tight around his shoulders, he said to Hank, "We got some yachts breaking their moorings in the harbor. The roads are getting blocked with fallen trees."

So far not much had been seen of tunnel or cave but small holes were uncovered where muskrats had been hiding. Once in a while a muskrat would pop out of the mud, look, and then scurry away from the tractor blade. The men with their own small shovels would endlessly dig, cleaning up after the tractor, and, as they became exhausted, fall out of line and immediately give their shovels to rested volunteers.

The trench had been widened to about ten feet, which allowed the bucket to load and retrieve its fill. This meant that as the trench lengthened, the walls were also longer and reached as high as ten feet. The men tried to reinforce them to keep them from collapsing by using two by four eight foot studs and plywood sheets jammed into the earth, with sandbags shoved against them.

A loud, boisterous voice called out, "Sammy, where the hell are you?"

Hank looked up to see John Duke, the chief reporter, editor, publisher, and owner of the River Sunday Sentinel, walking toward the site, camera slung over his shoulder. He had healthy white hair, long and flowing, and even though he was a contemporary of Pete in age, he climbed over the sandbags like a far younger man.

Duke had grown up in River Sunday and spent most of his newspaper career in Baltimore where he strived for but never achieved an editorial post on any of the city papers. He came home and bought the Sentinel when it was almost bankrupt and proceeded to keep it afloat with a mixture of exciting headlines and newspaper bluster. Hank thought people read the editorials as a game, to see what sort of a fool Duke was making of himself.

Duke could bluster. He was hard to outtalk, loud and opinionated, and fully capable of shouting down anyone who disagreed with him. He made a living from squeezing news from gossip. His followers, of dubious education Hank thought, paid to read the news he generated. Duke liked to tell stories, too, and if he had a saving grace it was his interest in the town, even though many times people would say he got story facts wrong. His knack for elaborating made his reporting more sensational than true. Even though Hank did not like him personally, he did enjoy, from time to time, Duke's highly embellished stories about local happenings.

Hank remembered one day Duke was at the garden shop, talking to his father. Duke got going on why he was a writer. He said, "I like to wring the meaning out of our simple lives."

His father, in his stolidity, pushed back his dark hair and scanned the puffed-up newsman in front of him. Then he lifted another sack of manure and said, in the practical way that he discussed most things, "I sure wish you luck with your wringing, Mr. Duke. Be careful, though, that you don't wring so hard you got no life left to report."

In developing a noteworthy issue in a small town like River Sunday, Duke had seized on the environmental. He promoted such loving care of wildlife that Hank sometimes wondered if the man had ever witnessed the hard side of nature. Had he ever got horse hornets attacking him after walking on their nest out in some cornfield?

Duke had increased his circulation noticeably in the past few years. He liked to report that the only war of the future was the war with nature. Most of his advertisers and readers were older persons who were retired and observed the world with conservative eyes. Many times he portrayed animals as far more worthy of attention than humans and greatly superior to humans. His newspaper was now receiving attention from a younger generation that had adopted the environmental crusade and he was often quoted on Baltimore television as a rural savant crying out with his message of saving the earth for the animals. The Federal Bureau of Investigation had even interviewed him because his newspaper had been found at the location of a bombing of a factory that used animals for testing new drugs. To him, when he talked of this interview, it was as a mark of his relevance, not of his participation in crime. This FBI interview was fodder for several weeks' worth of articles, and the FBI's letter of apology was framed and hung behind his desk.

Sammy, who appreciated Duke helping with fundraising for the fire department, waved to him from the tractor while preparing to run in for another load. Duke stopped and waited as Bob Johnny came up to him. Bob Johnny saw Duke as an accomplice in his never-ending public relations campaign for the Wilderness.

"It's Hank Green's boy," said Bob Johnny, obviously pleased that Duke had arrived, and pointed to Hank, who concentrated on his shoveling.

"I got that much from town," answered Duke, checking out the area. "What are the boy's chances?"

"No way to tell whether he's still alive," replied Bob Johnny, putting his shovel to work.

"People want to know," said Duke.

Pete tossed another shovelful. "Seems like most of the town is here already."

"The television people have been calling," said Duke, excitement in his voice.

"Come on, John," said Pete, one of the few people who called the newspaper man by his first name. "No need to tell people in Baltimore about a poor kid getting trapped in a cave."

"We got a story here," said Duke. "This swamp's against the boy, against the strongest team we could get together."

"I guess you're right," said Pete." If you don't do the story someone else will be in here and do it just as bad or worse." He called to Hank who was lifting his shovel. "All right with you, Hank?"

"Sure," said Hank tossing another load behind the sandbags. "Melissa likes publicity."

"OK, so tell me what happened," Duke said.

Pete rested his shovel and said, "I had seen them go by on their bicycles. Hopping ditches. It was a real nice afternoon before the storm come up."

"Hopping ditches?"

"That's what I call it. One of them rides into the ditch along the road and tries to hop the culvert at the lanes coming off the main road. I saw Bobby smack up his bike, get himself up and start riding again. I watched them go down to the dock. I heard the outboard start up."

"It was all right with me," said Bob Johnny. "The kids don't bother anything. They work for me sometimes, putting out corn for the geese."

"The clouds started to come up," Pete said. "The rain started, fine at first, but you could tell from the sky color we were in for something. I thought about taking my own boat out to search for them. Then I heard their engine, running wide out, coming in, fast. Could not really see it beyond the reeds."

"I guess you weren't around, Bob Johnny?" asked Duke.

"No, I was up to town. I heard the alarm go off and I followed the trucks out here right away."

Pete continued, "A few minutes later I was inside my house and heard knocking at the door and screaming. I opened the door and a gust of wind howled into the room and blew my newspaper into the air. I believe it might even have been your paper, John.

"Cathy was standing there, soaked, missing one of her shoes, yelling, 'He's caught down in a hole. It just fell in. The mound came down on him.'"

"We just found a kid's shoe," called one of the firemen from the trench. The shoe was passed over from the sandbag area to Pete. He held it up into the light.

"Can I have it back?" asked Cathy, tiny in Pete's large slicker which reached to the ground around her small body.

"I'll get a picture," said Duke. Pete waited while Duke adjusted his camera and snapped the photo.

Then Duke asked, "Robin Pond been here? She'll want to tell you how to save the muskrats inside the mound."

"No," said Bob Johnny, staring at the boats a hundred or more yards offshore. "I'm sure she's out there saving animals though," he said, pointing out into the darkness where boat lights twinkled and moved slowly in the surrounding darkness.

Hank could see another man climbing out of a newly arrived boat, photographic gear strapped over his shoulders, his hands carrying a large video camera. Behind him came a woman in a full-length windbreaker. She yelled into the wind, "I want to see John Duke, the editor of the River Sunday Sentinel."

"Well, we're right here for you," Duke called back, winking at Pete. "I'm John Duke."

She stopped, slightly out of breath. "Tawny Slight. I'm covering this story for Baltimore."

"You're not one of the regulars," said Duke.

"No way for them to get here from Baltimore," she replied. "With the winds, the helicopters can't cross the Bay. I was down on another assignment and my editor told me to come here right away."

"How much do you know about the situation?" asked Duke.

She caught her breath. "A little boy was trying to find an airplane wreck and got trapped in a cave-in."

She pulled out her notepad, shielding it from the drizzle. Duke put his hand under his chin and reviewed the young television reporter in front of him. "You're not from this part of the country, are you?"

She smiled. "California. I just started with Baltimore news."

"All right. Here you are," Duke said as he took charge and pointed to the team of firemen shoveling in the trench. "Sammy there on the tractor, he'll know the members of the rescue team. Hank Green, there with the shovel, he's the boy's father so he can tell you about the boy and his family. Pete Smithfield can tell you about the swamp. You being a stranger to River Sunday, if you want, I'll try to fill you in on local background, human interest, that kind of angle."

She nodded eagerly, her pad held up and ready in front of her face, the back of her writing hand brushing the paper from time to time to keep off the raindrops. Her photographer had begun to shoot pictures.

Cathy spoke up. "We were searching for the P47."

Tawny's eyes creased. "P47?"

Duke pointed to the twelve year old. "Cathy's one of the kids with Bobby Green when he got trapped. A P47 is a kind of World War Two fighter plane that crashed out here during the War. The kids come out to try to find it. Kind of a tradition."

"Tell me about the accident," she said.

"I'll tell her," said Pete. He went through what the firemen knew. She wrote fast, lifting her face to him from time to time as he explained.

When he had finished, she said, "Tell me more about this airplane they were hunting for."

Duke interrupted, "You should write about the woman pilot."

"A woman was lost out here?"

"Zinnie. Her proper name was Melusina Allingham, a member of one of our oldest families. She had been one of the first commissioned woman fighter plane pilots, ferrying planes around the cities on the East Coast."

"How did it happen?"

"Women weren't supposed to be in combat. However, on Easter Sunday in 1944, she risked her life when she was checking out a newly repaired fighter. She was flying over the ocean and spotted a German submarine. She radioed continuously the sub position from her unarmed plane as the Nazis tried to escape. She was wounded by fire from the U-boat. When she flew home, she got into a storm - one of the worst storms the area had ever seen. We call it the Easter Storm of 1944. Her last radio message indicated she was crashing into the Wilderness Swamp. End of story. She and her plane were never found."

"That's why these kids were out here, still trying to find her?" Tawny asked.

"Fifty years later, that's right. Zinnie was like a protector of the town, like a woman knight. People thought that she had finally destroyed the same enemy submarine which had blown up a tanker a few months before outside our harbor," said Duke.

As he worked, half listening to the newsman, Hank saw a thin black line undulating in the mound surface in front of him, like a hill and valley and hill again pattern. He had not noticed this before in the light brown color in front of him. It was a trace of darkness. He picked at it with his shovel.

"After the tanker sank, the town tried to get this submarine. A retired World War One Army general even sent his schooner after her. In the early days of the War the Navy and Coast Guard didn't have enough ships."

"A sailboat after a submarine?" Tawny blinked in disbelief.

"The son of this General was given command of the schooner and its crew, some of the town's best yachtsmen who were waiting for their call up for regular service."

"How were they going to attack it?" asked Tawny, jotting quickly.

"They had a machine gun the General got for them from the Maryland Armory in Baltimore and there were some depth charges. I understand they practiced shooting the machine gun out in the harbor. People would assemble on the wharfs at the harbor and watch."

"Wasn't much," said Sammy who was checking the tractor engine.

"So what happened?" she asked.

"The schooner met up with the submarine all right. When the sub aimed its big deck cannon at them, the General's son immediately ordered the machine gun thrown overboard along with the depth charges and their racks. Then he hoisted a white sheet from one of the crew's bunks.

"Unfortunately just as he hauled up the sheet, the jettisoned depth charges hit their level and exploded below the schooner. They threw up geysers. The Germans fired back and set the schooner on fire. A Nazi crew boarded and lined up the River Sunday people on deck. The soldiers made our people kneel and take a pledge to not shoot at any more German warships. Then they put them into the schooner lifeboat, set them adrift, and submerged the sub just as the schooner sank. The River Sunday crew finally came ashore in the breakers off Ocean City and took a bus home."

"That was the end of it, until Zinnie?"

"Yeah," said Duke.

"What happened when the crew got home?"

"Well there wasn't any parade. The General was quoted as saying, 'If I'd been there, I would have put a few rounds in the Krauts before they got me.' The town had his remark printed and stuck on the walls of stores around River Sunday."

"Like the saying *don't give up the ship*?"

"Like that," said Duke.

"Didn't mean a thing," said Sammy, climbing back up on the tractor. "Germans got a laugh and the man lost a good schooner." The tractor engine roared again.

"So Zinnie really got the town honor back," said Tawny.

"Yes," said Duke. "You can understand why people want to find her airplane."

Hank continued digging. More of the seams were appearing. Other men found them too. All had the same characteristics, three to five feet in length, and the curving pattern. Shovels cut through them and there was no extended seam. It was as if these were buried signs from the past. Reverend Blue would say they were a sign of the intelligent design. He wore a battery-powered necktie with little lights. He'd set them off and on to show his enthusiasm.

Chapter Five

Pete came up behind Hank as the tractor was backing away to dump another load. "Any more of the marks?"

Hank ignored him for a moment and turned to Charlie. "Charlie, you hear anything yet?"

Charlie shook his head. He continued to adapt and adjust his simple radio equipment. He'd placed microphones at various spots around the mound, which fed signals into the small tent where he had his gear. Charlie's idea, as he explained it to Hank, was similar to the way the Navy used radio direction finders to locate a ship at sea. He'd try to locate the source of the noise by observing the strength of the sound picked up by the microphones in various locations

Hank turned back to Pete. "About the marks. I did spot these on the wall where the tractor just scraped." Hank pointed to one of the lines with the tip of his shovel. "They are not like the marks the muskrats make."

Pete put his finger on the line and withdrew it, studying the residue. "Yeah, muskrats don't walk on the side of a hill like this and there are no prints that resemble little hands. Tell you what, I think that's rust."

"Rust?"

"Maybe there was a link steel fence along here and it got buried somehow."

Hank pushed his shovel into the ooze that the tractor had left behind. He lifted the heavy wet earth and threw it to his left so that it did not hit Pete. The muck splashed harmlessly into the marsh water outside the sandbags.

Hank said, "Jimmy used to tell Bobby about the muskrats."

Pete nodded. "Don't you worry about Jimmy. He understands what we got to do here."

"It's natural for him to be concerned," said Hank. "It's the graves of his people."

"Jimmy believes in the living more than the dead."

"You know, Bobby likes animals, too. Maybe Jimmy taught him that," said Hank. "Melissa wouldn't let him have any pets up there in that big old house. He had a cat at the store - an old alley cat that used to hang around my father."

"I tell you what, Hank. I miss your father planting his trees."

Hank thought about his father. One time he was at the kitchen table talking about his experiences as an immigrant. "I wasn't a Jew but they thought I was because of the way I talked. They thought all displaced people must be Jews," his father had said, drinking his coffee. His father would stir in several spoons of sugar, one after another, watching the grains fall into the black water.

His mother had looked over from the sink where she was washing dishes. "People here didn't like Jews right after the war and some of them still don't. You're going to hurt the business with your charity work."

"The rabbi came to me. I wanted to help him grow a garden at his synagogue."

"You gave him too many free plants, too many hours without getting paid," she had insisted before she had left the room. She was angry and had left them to eat their breakfast without her.

Pete interrupted Hank's memories. The old man dumped his shovel. "I remember the last one of those pines your father planted for Bobby out here."

"Yes. That was before Melissa took Bobby to her house. She had left me but Bobby still came around. Bobby'd come into the store with his nanny," said Hank. "The nurse would let him run around in the greenhouse. He'd ask my father all kinds of questions about the plants."

"I bet you liked that," said Pete.

"Yes. As far as the animals, I remember that Bobby loved the old cat best of all. 'Where's the cat?' he'd ask. 'Where's the cat, Daddy?' Then without waiting for me to tell him, he'd just take off hunting for it. He was an expert on that cat. Knew all its hiding places.

"There was one time in the store, Bobby wanted a particular toy. That was the only time I ever saw my father upset about giving the child anything."

"A toy?"

"The salesmen would bring in samples. My father went over everything. He was pretty particular. You've seen the toy room. There are a couple of shelves of things - games and the like for kids. On that day, some of them were in a pile on the floor by the cash register."

Hank stabbed with his shovel. "See there's some more of the dark lines in the soil."

Pete studied the marks. "Yep."

"I remember when Bobby held up a certain toy to show my father." Hank stopped. "It was a simple plastic toy, a little submarine. It was, of course, painted in military colors. When Bobby pressed it on the sides, the top of the conning tower would pop up and a little smiling man would come out."

"My father said to me, 'I should have thrown that away before Bobby found it.'

"'He just wants it for his bath,' I said, smiling.

"'I should have thrown it away,' he repeated, and walked away."

Pete said, "I don't think he was being mean. Your father loved the kid. What about the letter he left him?"

"Yeah, the letter," said Hank.

The tractor approached on its scooping run. They stepped back as the machine went into the trench to load.

Cathy had come up behind them, her large windbreaker rustling in the wind. "Will he be free soon?"

"Soon, honey," said Hank.

"It's so sad, both of them being out here in the Wilderness," said Cathy.

"You're talking about your great aunt being with Bobby," said Pete.

Cathy nodded, "She was like me."

"She wasn't a figure skater like you," said Hank.

"That's not really something I want to do. Daddy wants me to," she answered.

Hank shook his head, not speaking, but unable to understand why Will did the things he did.

Pete pulled another shovelful. "I can remember when Zinnie had a little plane here in River Sunday. She kept it at the same airport although the place wasn't much more than an unplanted field."

"You told me she'd take up passengers for rides on Heritage Day," said Cathy.

Pete rested his shovel, "She flew over in that plane. She called it an Aeronca. She'd buzz in from the direction of the Wilderness, in the afternoon, the late sun on her wings so bright you couldn't hold your eyes on her. You just heard the engine. Sometimes, depending on how she flew over, we'd see the shadow over the house as she passed, making up a cold breeze. Me and the wife, we'd wait for her flying over, like it was a blessing or something. That shadow, it always meant good luck to me."

"Did you ever go up flying with her?" asked Cathy.

"I did one time," he said. "Like you say it was on Heritage Day only a long time ago. The town wasn't as decorated as it is today, no floats in parades, that kind of thing."

"No fire trucks."

"Oh, yes," said Pete, pushing in his shovel again, "We had two fire trucks but they weren't as powerful as the ones we have today, the ones your father helped buy, Hank."

Cathy moved closer as she listened.

"Zinnia was just as pretty as you are, child. She had long hair, the same as you, only she was all grown up when I flew with her. She had a leather cap that fitted over the top of her head and goggles that she kept pulled back on the leather.

"They'd cleared a part of the highway outside of town for her to take off and land; cars that came along had to wait until she landed or took off.

"I stood out there with the others waiting my turn. The ride cost me fifty cents which was a good amount of money but it was something I had been anticipating."

"Were you scared?" asked Hank.

"I wasn't scared so much as I was wondering what I'd do if the bottom fell out of the plane. I had thoughts of holding on to the wheels underneath. That whole night before, I made up a plan to save myself, you see." He chuckled.

"The plane resembled a bathtub with little wheels under the engine. I climbed into my seat and Zinnie said, "You all set?" Before I could answer her, we were heading into the wind and first thing we were up in the air.

"The flight was pretty standard although I didn't realize that at the time. She flew up to about two or three hundred feet and began a slow circle around the town. Below I saw all the people on the highway and then I spied the courthouse and all the trees around it. She dipped the wing to a friend below in the courthouse square where the politicians were making speeches. I couldn't see who it was but she had a lot of friends. Then we came around over the slave monument. In those days it didn't have all the markers of the names of slaves living in River Sunday before the Civil War. It was just a pile of rocks. I recognized a friend fishing by the rocks and waved to him.

"Zinnie had the aircraft window open and the air blew in my face. It was cool up in the air. On the ground the day had been very hot like it always is in August. The air smelled fresh and the plane smelled of canvas and leather.

"When she came around to the highway again, we started down for a landing. I watched the instruments change as we descended. She had a little rosary in front of her, hanging from the dash. It was made of ivory, I remember. It swung back and forth.

"The front of the plane went up and the tail went down. We hit the road with a slight bump. All I could see in front was the propeller. Zinnie was observing around her as she moved the plane forward to the line of ticket holders.

"You had to clamber to get out of the machine. When I was standing beside the plane again, she asked, 'Pete, you like the flight?'

"'Yes, Ma'am,' I replied.

"'Being up there makes it all equal, you remember that,' she said. Then she reached in her pocket and gave me back my fifty cents. 'This one's on me,' she said."

Pete pushed his shovel harder into the mud. "That's how I recognized she was luck for me, that lady. I think she's always been lucky for this town, too, and the people in it."

"Kind of like an angel," Cathy said.

"Yes, an angel," said Pete.

Cathy said, "Like that song Bette Midler sang about the wind."

Chapter Six

Captain Steele, his flashlight waving, plodded through the marsh grass towards Hank and the others. He was an older man, the manager of the airport, but he still had energy in his eyes and retained the sharp chin of his youth.

Hank would never forget the wartime photograph displayed in the River Sunday drugstore window. Steele, silk scarf around his neck, and hat set back, stood with his crew beside his P47 fighter. Its metal side was covered with tiny neatly spaced swastikas, painted records of his aerial kills. Beside him stood his aircraft mechanic, with a massive bandolier of fifty caliber cartridges for the wing guns slung around his neck. All these men were young, grinning for the camera, and full of fight. "56th Wolf Pack" captioned the picture. Hank remembered these were the same words used by the Nazi submarine patrols.

Steele did not like Will Allingham and made this evident at every chance. The Captain refused to come to see or help design the parade model of the other P47 of town history, the plane belonging to Will's heroic aunt Zinnie.

This night, Steele still wore a cap in his cocky fashion even though it did not protect his face against the drizzling rain. He stood next to Hank and inspected the sandbag wall.

"That stake up there show where Bobby got trapped?"

Pete put down his shovel. "Yes."

The Captain pulled on some branches of bushes growing from the edge of the mound. They started to come loose in the soft earth spraying water and black soil over his hands. He quickly let go and rubbed his hands together to shake off the dirt.

"Any sign of life?" he asked.

"Plenty of muskrats," said Pete. "Charlie thought he might have heard something but that was awhile back."

The Captain turned to Hank. "How are you holding up?"

"I'll make it," said Hank.

"We've got high tide too with this storm getting stronger," said the Captain.

"What's the latest weather from the airport?"

"Main winds going to hit us hard," answered the Captain. "It's coming in almost the same track as the Easter Storm of 1944. Baltimore airport's closed up tight."

The Captain saw Sammy on the tractor and waved. Sammy stopped the machine and climbed down. He reached into his trousers pocket and handed Cathy's small piece of metal to the Captain.

"Here's why I called your cell," said Sammy. "Ever see anything like that before?"

The Captain examined it by the light for a few minutes, turning it from one side to the other and holding it up. Then he nodded to Sammy.

"You said you didn't think it was a Native American religious object. Jimmy might not agree but I think you're right about that, Sammy. I could swear that I've seen something else just like this. Let me get back to my office. I can figure it out."

Pete's brow creased. "Remember, we haven't got a lot of time."

"I'll be quick as I can." He nodded at Hank. "Sorry about all this."

Sammy said, "Say, Captain, that piece of metal you got there. Don't get too excited about it."

"Why?"

"Since I called you, I have been thinking. Might be a fishing lure. Raccoon or muskrat might have found it out in the marsh and dragged it up here."

Captain Steele studied the metal again, flipped it in his hand, and nodded. "I'll keep that in mind, Sammy."

Pete spoke up. "What about those black marks you spotted in the mud, Hank? Show him."

The Captain turned his head. "What lines, Hank?"

Hank pointed to one of the wavy seams. "They keep coming up and then disappear. They aren't made of much. Just like a little bit of color and then they are gone."

"What do you think, Pete?" asked the Captain as he tapped the seam with his finger.

"I told him I thought it was rust," answered Pete.

The Captain scraped out a sample, wrapped it carefully into a handkerchief, and put it into his pocket. "Pete, you might have something here."

"What?"

He shook his head. "I'll be back as fast as I can." He walked back to the boats.

Mrs. Pond had run her boat near the shoreline as she gathered wild creatures.

"I wonder what she thinks Bobby's chances are," said Hank as he watched her.

Pete said, "Mrs. Pond would be the last one to give up on anything. Folks start giving up on Bobby and you'll see her come in for the last try. She's that way. Helps the hopeless."

"I guess I never saw that side of her," said Hank.

"Hope you don't have to."

"Stop the tractor," Bob Johnny yelled. "You hit one of them."

Sammy slowed the machine and began to lift the bucket up. At the top, on the sharp edge, half of the body of a muskrat bled on the steel, and then slithered off into the mire below.

Sammy called out, the engine quieter, "What you say?"

Bob Johnny reached under the bucket and held up the dead muskrat. Sammy nodded and pushed forward the throttle.

"Try to be more careful," said Bob Johnny.

Sammy nodded again. As he did, Bob Johnny tenderly put the dead animal by the side of the trench. This was the first real emotion Hank had seen on Bob Johnny's face since Hank had arrived at the mound.

Cathy and Richard walked carefully across the soft top of the mound on small pieces of plywood strapped to their shoes.

She explained, "Richard said we could use the wood like snowshoes. He was right."

Richard nodded.

Tawny, Duke, and the photographer began photographing the two children. Cathy sat and took off her boards to clean the muck from them. "I can tell you the Nanticoke legend of a giant muskrat that lives in this mound," she said to Tawny.

Her father, Will, was stuffing sandbags nearby. "Don't tell her what Jimmy Swift told you, Cathy."

Tawny waved to Will. "I want to hear."

"Cathy, I said no," her father shouted.

Cathy spoke up. "Jimmy told me the big muskrat's name was Sachem. It means big chief in the Nanticoke language."

"Sachem," repeated Tawny. "Has anyone ever seen this giant Sachem?"

Cathy stared defiantly at her father as she spoke. "Only one person. At least the story goes that he must have seen him. Anyway he was killed by the creature."

"Killed?"

"There were these French settlers who were sent to River Sunday by the British. They were Acadians from Nova Scotia. One of them, a man named Francois D 'Argent was a trapper and he decided to hunt the Wilderness for muskrat. The Nanticoke tribal members, who were few even by that time, advised him he could hunt in most of the swamp. However, he should leave alone this area where the burial mound was because Sachem, the giant white muskrat, lived there.

"This man was brave and he had hunted in the far north in Canada for beaver. He asked the Nanticokes if anyone had ever seen Sachem and no one could say that they or anyone they knew had seen the big muskrat. Francois declared that he was not afraid of any muskrat much less one that was a legend. He set out his traps in this section of the swamp.

"In the morning when he left River Sunday to check his traps, he promised that he would be back by evening with many muskrats. When evening came he was not back. Several days went by and he still did not return. Pretty soon his friends, some of the other Acadians, got together a search party and went out to the Wilderness.

"When they got near to the edge of the swamp, they came across a solitary Nanticoke man, who was old and feeble, his skin dry and taut to his bones as if he were already dead. He was dressed only in a breechclout and moccasins and smoked a long pipe. His body was covered with fresh bright red clay. He asked them where they were going. They explained that they were looking for their friend and asked him if he had seen the trapper. The old man replied that he had seen a trapper who was going into the marsh to check his traps. He warned him not to go but the man went anyway.

"'Which way did he go?' the searchers asked.

"The old man pointed toward the section of the swamp where the mound was located.

"They took several canoes and went out to the island. There they found a stack of broken muskrat traps. Beside them was the straw hat that Francois had been wearing. All around were the footprints of a big animal, and from what they could see, the marks matched those of muskrats. However they were large."

She paused and whispered, "Blood was everywhere."

Then Cathy went on, louder. "They searched all over the mound and paddled for several miles around the small islands nearby in the Wilderness. They couldn't find him."

Tawny stared at the young girl.

Cathy continued, "About a year later, a rusty hatchet was found on the road to the swamp. It turned out to have belonged to the trapper."

"So he was killed by the monster?" asked Tawny.

"Yes," she said. "Maybe others saw Sachem, too, but were eaten by him before they could talk."

"Did anyone ever see the old man again?"

"No," she said, "Jimmy says he was the spirit of Chief Nanticoke who came up from his grave in kindness to warn the Frenchman to leave Sachem alone."

"No one has ever trapped muskrats in this area?"

"Not near the mound. My family in their fur business only trapped at the other end of the swamp. My Dad has his hunting places there now."

Tawny put down her pad. Cathy's face was still serious. The reporter's mouth was frozen in a twisted expression between belief and disbelief at the tale.

Will said, "They get these stories from Swift. I want the school children to study real history. I'm sorry, Tawny."

"I'd like to meet this Jimmy," Tawny said.

Bob Johnny said, "He'll be here when he wants to be."

Cathy's face was solemn. "Just because you don't see Sachem doesn't mean you shouldn't believe he lives here. Jimmy says lots of things are true that we don't see. I think Sachem's taking care of Bobby right now. "

Chapter Seven

The firemen who had been on the job since the beginning were covered with filth. They were battle-worn and exhausted like soldiers after an attack. They sat on the sandbag walls for brief respites for coffee or a smoke.

Meanwhile the wall of sandbags around the mound grew higher. Yet the bags did not stop all the water. Trickles of water broke through in spots and shot out into the walkway in small streams.

Hank did not stop for long when he rested. He would get back up and work even faster, his back not rested, always aching, his arms sore from lifting the full shovels.

Sammy had given the tractor to one of the other men. He was standing near Hank and put down his cell phone.

"Melissa's on her way," he said.

"Where was she anyway?" asked Hank, caring more because she was Bobby's mother than any remaining personal interest he had in his former wife.

"She was driving to town coming out that lane from her house. Her car slid into a ditch. Her farmer just got her out and she called to say she's coming soon."

"I forgot," said Hank. "They had her Easter Party today. The Easter punch is strong stuff."

Sammy turned to Will. "That right, Will?"

Will said, "I wasn't there."

The others exchanged glances at Will's comment. They had thought he went everywhere with Melissa.

"Melissa sounded all right to me," Sammy said.

Melissa arrived about ten minutes later. It was a dark afternoon in the rain. As she was getting off the boat, Hank could only see her raincoat, which was her father's old yachting windbreaker, the yellow hooded canvas that had always been too big for her. He knew why she was wearing it. She took it along as an icon whenever she was worried. She liked to say wearing the jacket made her feel her father was near. Hank thought it was another of her fantasies, because her father had visited her only a few times in her life. The General had told Hank that the last person who had worn that jacket was one of his son's London girlfriends. It came addressed to Melissa in an international packet stuffed with some of her father's other belongings. That was several years ago, the year he drowned in his last sailboat race, off the coast of England.

Hank thought of Pete's words, repeating the same observation the old man had been saying to him for years. "Melissa's like a flower. A flower that you should not touch," said Pete."Pretty, fragile and followed in autumn with a gnarled seed pod."

He spaded another load. As he did he noticed the dirt had changed color. It was lighter. He motioned to Sammy and held up the full blade for him to see. Sammy, who was starting back to take over the tractor, stopped and looked. He nodded with a grin. "That's drier dirt from inside the mound where the water ain't got yet. That's where Bobby is, we hope."

Hank remembered those early days with Melissa at her home. He'd hear from inside her house, "Melissa, who's here to see us?"

"It's Hank, Grandpa."

"Well, bring the man in here. He probably needs a drink."

Melissa would lead him into the big library where the General sat in a great stuffed chair, books and papers spread around him, and his guest from Baltimore usually sitting on his lap or kneeling at his feet. The driver of the Cadillac in the driveway was long legged, about thirty-five years old, and very feminine, blonde, and expensive.

"You know everybody, Hank," the General would say.

Hank would say, "Yessir."

Then the General would talk about Hank's father and the mansion gardens. Hank's father spent many hours with the General working on the trees or shrubs helping them survive in the blistering Chesapeake summer sun.

"Your father was out the other day and saved my old oak tree down in the front walkway. Man sure as hell knows his trees. You going to take over the business someday?"

The General would always ask him that question as though he thought it was the natural thing for Hank to do, as if he were complimenting him in some way by suggesting that his father had enough faith in him to do so.

Hank's father's opinion of Melissa, on the other hand, was limited to his one comment, "I do not understand why she doesn't like flowers."

Hank would then joke with his father, "She does like the General."

His father would reply, "You aren't the General, son."

Hank's mother would just close her lips and murmur, "It'd be nice if you married into all that money."

Sitting there, though, in the library at the mansion, Hank would say to the General, "I'd like to work more in the store but my father thinks I need to go to college first."

The General would say, "College is a good idea. Might consider West Point."

"Yes, sir," Hank would say, as Melissa brought him a large glass of whiskey and ice.

"Military is not for most men. I know that." He'd address Hank then wistfully as if he expected him to stand and salute, as if he wanted to recommend Hank right away for a cadet application.

Hank would say, "I want to study horticulture."

The General then said, and it was almost word for word each time the subject came up, "A lot to be said for that, Hank. Your father understands what's good for you, even though he's not a military man."

This night, the Cadillac had been there, and the General said to his friend, "I personally never did like college. I didn't like the assholes who were teaching the courses. Always felt like smacking them up the side of the head." The General would throw back his head and laugh deep and long. Then he'd sit up and say, "What do you say about that, lady?" And he had rubbed the thin knees of his guest with his large hand, the other hand holding his whiskey.

She answered, throwing back her long blonde hair so that it brushed against the General's face, and speaking with the tough voice of a professional, practiced by years of yelling after patrons who didn't pay her, "I knew a college professor once."

"Tell us about him," the General had said. Then, before she spoke, he had boomed out, "Melissa, get Hank a refill of bourbon. That's what a man drinks."

The guest pouted her lips and said, in a soft voice, "Professors have awful small dicks, and they always call them penises."

The General had set back his head and laughed deeply, Melissa and Hank laughing with him. The General had said, "I think you mean to say, penii."

"No, I mean penises," the blonde said, straightening the General's necktie.

"Melissa, you settle it," the General had said. "Penises or penii?"

Melissa had said, her eyes at the edge of her glass as she faced her grandfather, "I don't know, Grandpa."

The last time he was in that library, three years ago, he and Melissa had their big fight. Bobby was asleep upstairs. Hank sat in the same chair he always sat in. Melissa walked back and forth, drink in hand, talking to him about the failure of their marriage.

"You're cute, Hank. You always have been. You're just not handsome. I want someone handsome for Bobby."

"My appearance used to mean a lot to you," Hank had replied.

"Maybe you should have married Betty," she said. "She's more your type. She likes to call you Greenie."

"Betty is my friend," he had said.

"I guess that's the problem, Hank. We're not friends any more." Then she had stopped walking and stared at him. "My father used to sit in that chair when he came to visit." Hank had met her father one time, years before, when he had visited River Sunday on his ocean yacht. There was a party on the boat and Hank was invited. The General was in the saloon, entertained by several women. When Hank approached, the General nodded and waved him on to the stern to find Melissa. She was near her father in the cockpit. There were several other women there, bikini clad, tanning them in the midday sun. After the party Melissa had mentioned that she was glad to see her father and happy to meet some of his friends. She had said, "They all love him so much, don't they?"

That day in the library when their marriage was being dissolved, Hank had shifted in the chair and said, "You think I'm your father?"

"No, no, I didn't mean that," she had said and began walking again. "Maybe that's the problem."

"What?"

"I realized that you could never be my father."

Then she quickly said, "I want Bobby to stay with me."

"He's my son, too," Hank replied.

"I know that and he loves you," she had said.

"Why do you want to hurt him?" Hank asked.

"Hurt him? Living in an upstairs room over a greenhouse isn't hurting him?"

"So that's it," Hank had said. He had gotten angry then.

"Your mother wanted him to move out here, you realize that," she had said.

"I didn't."

"Your father and the General agreed."

"I guess that made it final, didn't it?" said Hank.

"They all wanted him to have every advantage."

"That meant spending your grandfather's money on him."

"You never liked that idea. You wanted him to be poor, Hank."

"I was loved when I was a boy. I wanted him to have that."

She had become furious. "You think I don't love him."

Hank had said, "Loving him is different than spending money on him, Melissa."

"Get out of my house," she had said then, and he had left. Since Bobby was already asleep, he left also without his son. A few weeks later, Melissa's lawyers managed to convince the River Sunday judge that Hank had deserted his wife and son that night.

Hank remembered the last time he drove up to the mansion, only a few months ago, and parked in the same spot he had in earlier years. The bushes were different, put in by a firm from Baltimore at great expense. Melissa never gave Hank any direct business. The firm came by often to get plants from Hank because he was local and because the firm knew he had better and cheaper plants than they had. Why, they told Hank, put in their plants when his were just as good? Meanwhile Melissa paid twice as much for the plants.

He saw that a party was going on inside and so he walked around to the kitchen. At the kitchen door was a little porch where he and Melissa used to sneak out and sit for hours. He walked into the kitchen and several men and women, black and white, most of whom he knew and greeted, were preparing plates of various foods for the party.

He said "I just wanted to leave a check for Melissa." One of the black women smiled and disappeared into the dining room and in a moment Melissa came through the door, beautiful in her gown, her eyes flashing anger,

"What in the hell are you doing here? I'm having a party."

"I brought out Bobby's money."

"God damn you, Hank, just mail me the money."

Then, behind her flowing dress, Hank saw the small head of Bobby, dark hair and full face, and the same blue eyes that he and his father shared, beaming up at him. When Melissa noticed Bobby, she pushed him behind her, her silk rustling.

Bobby, his face red, his hands clenching, had pulled away and disappeared back into the other room, quickly and quietly. Melissa, in turn, stared at Hank as though he were a person she wanted out of her life forever. Hank put the check on the kitchen counter, then moved carefully from the room and out the back door. With the noise of the party blaring out the old mansion windows, he walked around to the front where his truck was parked among the bright sports cars of the guests.

Tonight, here in the swamp in this rescue of their son, Hank was together with Melissa again, for better or for worse. The rain had started up again. Melissa talked with Pete as he filled her in about the progress of the rescue. Her face reddened with anger. After a few moments, she broke away from Pete and went up to Will who was shoveling at the side of the mound several yards away from Hank.

She stared at Will. "The men told me how upset you were about your fences being cut. God, you are an asshole."

Will gazed at her, as if he were thinking of something else, his jacket and tie filthy. He said nothing.

Hank looked at him, realizing Will would always be "Single Shot Will."

Cochise scampered by Melissa, and she shouted, "Damn these rats!" That was another thing about Melissa, Hank remembered. She hated animals like the old General had. The farm he bought had been a prosperous dairy producer and he got rid of all the animals. Grain crops were all that grew on that farm. As he said to Hank's father, "Any wild animals that come on my farm, hunting season or not, they'll get shot and eaten for my dinner."

Melissa pulled her windbreaker up over her and walked toward Charlie's radio tent. "Charlie, tell me, what I can buy or send for to help you?"

"You could stop this storm so's we can get some better radio equipment over from Baltimore."

She was grim. "Pete said you heard one noise you thought was Bobby?"

He suddenly held his hands hard on his earphones.

Her face was tight. "Anything?"

Charlie nodded, pursing his lips to ask her to be quiet.

After a moment, Charlie said, "I just heard it again. I heard another thump sound. Let me listen." He adjusted the radio dials as Hank and Pete came over.

After a few more moments, he said, "Still quiet."

"You heard something. That's new," said Hank.

"Only one of the microphones picked it up. That one was placed in a hole down at the far end from the trench."

Then from out in the swamp Hank heard trees squeaking from their trunks rubbing against each other as they bent down. He saw the searchlights mounted around the perimeter begin to shake back and forth. A bigger gust, much bigger than the others, hit then, water rising out of the swamp and hurling at him and the others in stinging droplets. Sudden rain came down, making the darkness overpower the wavering lights. Hank reached out for Melissa to try to protect her from the torn reeds and small twigs that were snapping through the air. She stood back from him, holding her coat over her head.

Sammy shouted, his voice almost lost in the shriek of the gale. "Get the men back from those pines until these gusts let up."

Chapter Eight

Men and equipment were blown about the mound. Nothing held tight to the ground in the slop. The men had to clutch for supports against the gusts but none existed in the flimsy reeds. The trees were in danger, too, bent far over. The firemen's supplies, boxes, and equipment slid down the sides of the mound and tore into the sandbag walls. The next gust began with a roaring sound and ripped at Hank's feet, making him stumble. As he fought the energy, a flash of light broke over the mound lighting its surface like small flames. He was knocked to the ground and cold water spattered his face. The noise of the thunder following the lightning strike tumbled around him.

Sammy yelled, "She's coming down!"

The tree cracked in half. The top of the burning pine began to topple, shifting toward the trench. Sammy jumped from his idling tractor as the first part of the tree barely missed the machine and tumbled into the trench. Two of the firemen avoided the crashing branches by scrambling away from the sandbags. Twigs and pine cones, like stinging missiles, flew through the air.

With a final crash and tearing sound as one of its larger branches snapped, the rest of the pine came to rest against the sandbags. Its remaining limbs reached down into the dug trench and pinned a firemen. He screamed in pain, his leg held tight under the wet timber.

"Get him out," yelled Sammy, pulling at the closest part of the tree. "Get him out from under that tree!"

The foresters began sawing the tree trunk, their chainsaws screaming.

Pete called out, "Keep an eye on the other pines. They'll all come down."

Hank clambered toward the screaming fireman. Behind him, Sammy ordered his men to drop their shovels and help cut back the branches. He crawled further in the muck toward the fireman. The trapped man was one of Sammy's best ladder men. He had been at the garden shop just a week ago to get flowers for his wife.

Hank dropped as near to him as the tree would allow. "You're going to be all right. We're going to get you free."

"Hank, I'm in a damn mess, ain't I?"

The man was beginning to shake. A nearby fireman removed his rain coat and handed it to Hank. Hank in turn pushed it up between the branches and over the man.

"Sammy," Hank called. He was beginning to feel closed in.

"Right here, Hank. What's it like?"

"He's going into shock. Hurry up."

Sammy was on his cell phone, "Who's this? You get your ass in that ambulance. I don't care how bad the road is."

Tackle was attached between two of the still standing loblollies to raise the fallen trunk.

Pete looked up. "Careful. Those ropes might pull the others down too."

Sammy's eyes were serious. "They know what they're doing."

Another fireman came down and lay beside Hank to help him pull the man back as soon as the tree was lifted from the pinned leg. The tree inched upward. The other pines to which the tackle was attached bent with the strain.

"More," directed the fireman, signaling with his arm, "Bit more, and pull him out."

"Bring the stretcher," called Hank. An ambulance parked on shore near the Park Ranger's office held the paramedics that waited for Bobby. One of the attached loblollies began to crack under the strain, just like Pete had predicted.

"Hurry," yelled Sammy.

"He's out," said Hank, helping the others lift the fireman ahead of him and climbing up behind him. The foresters eased up the ropes on the other trees. The split seam up the side of the other pine stopped and did not break any further than halfway up the tree.

"Good work. Let's get him up to Pete's place until the paramedics get over here." said Sammy.

"Sammy, we got to do it all again," one of the men called.

"All right. We all know our jobs," said Sammy. He got on the tractor and the engine roared up again.

Hank saw strange shaped and colored clamshells embedded in the wall. He studied the surface wondering when he would find the tunnel that Bobby had entered. Hank pulled at some of the loose soil. A large chunk of earth slid loose and fell against his body, submerging his legs and waist, soaking into his shirt. He tried to move and could not, knowing that he had trapped himself. His brain sensed that the walls were coming at him. They were not, this was only a small slide, but he could not fight the fear. He panicked and flailed at the walls around him. Finally, with the last of his energy he managed to pull himself free and crawled out of the trench, just as the other men got to him. He stood in the open black air and rain, nausea tearing at him.

"You'll be all right," said Pete, knowing what the matter was and trying to help Hank stand.

"You can't know," Hank said. "It almost got to me."

"You did well."

"The fear I have when things crowd in on me. It won't go away," he said to Pete. "I worry that, in a clutch, I won't be able to help Bobby."

Sammy ran the tractor forward, scooping up some of the fallen muck, his head constantly checking the other trees. As he stopped on his reverse run and shifted gears, he yelled down to Hank, "Jimmy's spirits."

"What?" asked Hank.

"I think there are bad spirits are living in here. I'm convinced of it. We don't have no luck."

At that moment, the wind howled again and more thunder crashed.

"Damn, here she comes again," said Sammy.

"That lightning may hit my tractor," said Will.

"You mean you're worried about me being being struck while on the metal tractor, ain't you, Will?" said Sammy, staring hard with his sarcasm at Will.

More trench walls collapsed as the firemen tried to remove the last of the tree. The walls turned fluid and swirled, tumbling the carefully stacked sandbags and rendering much of the work of the last hours useless. On the trench floor split sandbags fell in wild directions with mire leaking down on them from the sagging walls. Thin streams of water started to flow out from the mound face itself.

"You want to help me run ashore for more gear, Hank? I could use you," called a fireman in his boat, holding the shore with his foot as he idled the engine.

"Yes," Hank said, as he climbed aboard. He knew what he had to do. The rain was harsh with the gusts. Large swells were running in the shallow stretch they had to cross to the mainland.

Sammy waded out to Hank. The chief was coughing more.

"Take a few minutes, Chief. You need to get some rest," said Hank.

Sammy spat. "The men need me. You fetching Mudman?"

Hank nodded. "I should have gone for him before."

Sammy said, "I don't mind telling you, I wish your father was here." He put his hand on Hank's arm. "Say to Mudman I could use him. You probably won't get through. The roads are blocked. Anyway, try it. Take my sedan with the siren." He handed Hank the keys.

Betty came down to the water behind Sammy. "I'll go with you," she offered.

Hank shook his head. "Better if Mudman talks just to me."

She stopped. Then her face showed that she understood that Mudman would talk to Hank and no one else. She raised her hand in a wave to wish him luck.

"I'll be back," said Hank, as the fireman gunned the outboard.

As the boat ran out in a broad circle, it passed the dim shapes of animal rescue boats, several of them, their running lights bobbing. The men and women aboard were bent in concentration on their work, pulling the creatures from the water and stowing them safely for the trip to shore. They leaned toward the wind, shadows of their figures in rain jackets and umbrellas moving up and down as the swells tore at their craft. Hank could not see their faces in the darkness but he was sure that Robin Pond and Jimmy Swift were there. One boat resembled the profile of Jimmy's long wooden rowboat with baskets piled in the center and a tiny engine at the stern. Another was similar to the Pond motorboat, a high-sided fiberglass machine with a central control panel and twin powerful engines.

The view of the mound became blocked by tall reeds growing out of floating islands. Jimmy had told him it was a place of death and of honor. His people especially honored the Nanticoke chief of legend who had lost his son fighting the English. Now only Jimmy came to pray for that hero.

The boat turned into another inlet and a glimmer came through the reeds from the big searchlights where the men worked. The light and the vibrations of the motor stirred old memories. They reminded him of a long time ago, of the child he had been. He felt the tremble in his small hand when he hit a big stick on the oak floor at his home. In those days, the other children talked of wartime terror and a burning tanker turning night into day on the town horizon. He was once again the little boy who raced around the dining room in the postwar years with a stick, telling his father he'd protect him from the Nazi invaders. He's say in as loud a voice as he could muster, "If that old dirty Nazi U-boat ever comes near River Sunday again, I'll knock it down."

The Fleetwood Mac song about landslides also came into his mind, keeping time with the slaps of the hull against the swamp water. Hank mouthed the few words he remembered, the spray smacking against his face as the boat pushed into the waves. He hoped his boy might hear him somehow from deep inside the mound and know his father was near and would somehow protect him.

Chapter Nine

Hank concentrated on controlling Sammy's big red sedan on the high-crowned back roads. The way to Mudman's trailer home was through River Sunday. The town itself was clear of fallen trees and branches, although there were large ponds of water flecked with fresh green leaves flooding parts of the streets. He went by the Jewish temple, then Reverend Blue's fundamentalist chapel, and finally the Catholic Church, all dark and deserted. Going down Strand Street, the main avenue through town, and past the waterfront, Hank could see frothy waves smashing over the docks. Asphalt and wood shingles from the colonial style storefronts were flying and battering the few cars parked along the curbs. The traffic lights, hung across the streets on bouncing wires, blinked yellow announcing danger. The light moved shadows wildly across the glass of the store fronts. When he reached the highway outside town, the road was deserted. Even Lulu's Motorboat, the neon-lit stripper bar that was usually open for the locals and the tourists traveling to the ocean resorts, was in darkness.

After crossing the highway, Hank entered a small dirt road where he had to slow down to avoid skidding on the wet gravel. At the side of the road the ditches were already filled with rain water and had their own little waves that overflowed and forced Hank to drive to the center of the high crown road. Mudman's trailer was up a side lane, tucked between groves of loblolly pines and large magnolia trees and surrounded by freshly plowed fields. Mudman's father, deceased for some time, had used this metal home for many years as a shelter for well-digging crews at construction sites. Mudman had converted it into a house for himself and Cincy. Parked next to it was a brand new blue well-drilling truck with a carefully lettered white sign on the truck door, Mudman Drilling Company, River Sunday, Maryland.

Years ago, Hank and Mudman went south on leave after Army training for Vietnam. They were two young men in Army dress, with shining brass for the return home after the graduation parade. They skipped off the Army bus and hitchhiked to Florida to have some fun. Mudman said to Hank many times afterward that the best thing he ever did was that trip. When they got to Florida, they entered a roadside store along a south Everglades highway to buy a cold soda. That was the day Mudman met Sincere, Cincy for short. She was a pretty girl, thin with a pug nose, long dark hair, and, on that day, she wore a baggy green cotton dress with drawings of the constellations on it. She worked as a counter girl and had a small table near a bright window where she would sit and make spare change reading fortunes. She took them home to her apartment, a one-room affair, and they stayed a week. They went to the beach each day, a skinny dipping place she knew, where they could smoke pot and drink and lay in the sun. At night they would go to the local places with her friends, in a truck she borrowed from the storeowner, places where the war was not discussed. When their leave was over, when it came time to go back to base, Mudman didn't want to leave her.

Approaching Mudman's trailer, Hank thought about the night the two of them left for Vietnam. His father drove them to the bus station in River Sunday. The older man shut off the engine and turned to the both of them, saying that the best soldiers don't ask questions. The men who argue are a liability to the team, he said, and get put on the most dangerous missions in hopes that they will get killed and the outfit will be rid of them.

Hank remembered turning to Mudman after they said goodbye and were leaving town on the bus. He said, "Daddy learned all that stuff when he was in the underground."

Hank followed his father's advice, kept his mouth shut, and learned how to survive. Mudman had a tougher time than Hank because he argued with the officers. When they got in country, Hank drew mostly guard duties. Mudman was assigned to dangerous patrols, including the one where he had to machine gun several Viet Cong women and children.

A year later, on the day when he and Mudman came home, they were in the cab driving into River Sunday from the bus station. Mudman said that he was taking all his mustering out pay and going to Florida to get Cincy.

The next day, he and Hank went out to the Ford dealer in River Sunday. Mudman bought a new convertible for cash and told Hank he was going to get rid of the rest of his Vietnam money; spend it as quick as he could. He said it was money from evil. Then he left town. When he came back Cincy was with him. Whether they ever actually got married, Hank did not know. That kind of formality did not seem important to either of them. Mudman and Cincy did not have children. Mudman said and she agreed that they did not want to take the chance that their babies might grow up to be soldiers for the next war.

Hank knocked on the aluminum door and Cincy opened it.

"I saw you drive in," she said in a soft accent.

Mudman sprawled asleep with no clothes on in his chair in front of a large television. A beer, unopened, was in his hand. A shrapnel scar showed where the black hair would never grow back on the left side of his chest.

"He's been asleep for a while. I'll have to wake him up and get him to bed," she said. She was naked too. The two of them never wore clothes unless she was telling fortunes with a customer or they had to go to town or work. Any other time, Hank would have taken his clothes off and sat with them. Melissa used to come along with him in those first years they were married before Bobby came along and before she inherited all her money. She would sit around with the rest of them, naked too, drinking beer out of tall bottles. She called it the sunshine club of River Sunday.

These two people, both of whom Hank loved, seemed to welcome nudity as a way to be separate from the humanity around them. Cincy said she was "without any gifts from the world outside her flesh" and as she described herself, "fully awake to everything real that surrounded her." Mudman in his ever present melancholy, going back as far as his childhood dissatisfaction before the war, claimed he had to be naked because he was getting "close to being planted," to his final state inside a coffin. He constantly told Cincy he was going to die. How they managed to coexist, with one happy and one sad, Hank did not understand, but they stayed together. When Melissa got her inheritance, she stopped visiting Mudman and his wife. Cincy was always asking about her. She often remarked to Hank that she did not understand why Melissa was no longer her friend.

Hank blurted quickly what had happened to Bobby. Cincy's face was downcast as she listened.

"I dreamed last night that something had happened to a friend. I didn't expect it was Bobby," she said.

"I've got to get back to the Wilderness," Hank said.

Cincy turned her head back toward Mudman. "Hank's here."

"It ain't right," Mudman said, waking. He moved his head and saw Hank.

His eyes had closed again, but he said, in his gruff voice, "Hank, I'm going to sell all my equipment and truck and leave the area. Let someone else do the well digging around here."

Then he mumbled something, his eyes still closed.

"We do got enough money," said Cincy, as Mudman began to snore.

She continued, "We got word yesterday that one of his Vietnam friends in the shelter up in Baltimore killed himself."

"What happened?"

"The vet left a note. Said the pills didn't help any more."

Hank studied his old friend Mudman's face twitching in sleep as if his mind were talking to itself. Hank fell back into a chair, the exhaustion overwhelming him.

"You got to rest, Hank," Cincy whispered. She was right. He was tired. He closed his eyes and dreamed of himself and Mudman as children, Bobby's age, playing at the General's annual Easter Party. Hank's parents were sitting with the General on the overlooking porch on green rockers. They held drinks, his mother with her "old fashioned" whiskey and his father with the German beer he loved. His father advised how to care for the General's boxwood garden, the General twisting his long mustache as he listened. The children, fifty of them of all ages invited from the Allingham School, running among boxwood, finding the painted eggs hidden among the branches and roots. He and Mudman and Melissa searched and Betty tagged along. Will hunted alone, intently pushing and shoving other kids as he dove under the huge overgrown box bushes, trying to find more than anyone else. The general insisted two of the eggs be hollowed and money placed inside. "Money makes it worthwhile for these kids," he'd say.

Mudman was invited because he went to the Allingham School. Otherwise, because of his father's dubious character, he would have been relegated to a lower social status. The school was the social leveler in River Sunday, making rich white and poor white equal and, in Bobby's generation, black talking to white.

Hank's head jerked alert. Cincy was trying to talk to Mudman but he was sound asleep. She sat on the floor beside her husband and rubbed his feet.

"You wake up, honey. It's your friend. Lord, it's the only friend you got in this town. You wake up."

Hank stood up.

She said, "I'll keep trying on him. I will sure try to get him to come help you, I will sure try."

Then, as Hank got into his car she ran out into the drizzle, still naked, and stood by the passenger window.

"I forgot to tell you inside," Cincy said. "I dreamed last night. I saw animals too. That's the way I know he is going to be all safe." She reached into the car and squeezed his hand.

As he drove the fire department sedan away, she stayed there, her right hand shielding her face against the rain. When he scanned the rear view mirror, the paleness of her bare body blended with the nearest circle of her white daffodils.

Stronger gusts beat on the sedan as he drove back through River Sunday towards the Wilderness. At the harbor Hank saw a newly careened yacht, its mast askew, that had dragged its anchor and smashed into the main pier. Lights flashed near the hull as some marina workmen scurried to save it from tearing itself apart against the pilings.

As he approached the turnoff to the swamp, he saw a new police barricade.

The officer in charge recognized him and waved him through. All along the entry road, cars were scattered, some with empty boat trailers. Deserted rescue trucks from nearby towns added to the frenzy to get to the scene. Hank noticed the television truck too, with its oversize station letters on the side and the antennas.

When he reached the dock, he saw several boats in the water, ferrying sandbags and personnel to and from the accident site. Two of the boats were marked Maryland State Police. He did not recognize the policemen who were in charge of the boats. They stopped him from getting into a boat that was loading. One of the officers, a tall man, asked him for identification. Hank's face was lighted in the officer's flashlight.

A voice called from behind Hank. "It's all right, Sergeant. The man is the father of the trapped boy. I'll take him out."

It was Captain Steele. "Come on, Hank."

Hank climbed aboard behind the Captain and the boat started away from the pier.

"I have an idea to share with you guys when we get out to the island," said Captain Steele. He lifted up the worn leather briefcase he was carrying. "I got a hunch about this whole thing."

Chapter Ten

Captain Steele walked ahead of Hank as they approached the mound. During Hank's absence, the digging had progressed only a few feet further into the hill, as the mud trench continued to collapse back into the trench.

"Sammy," shouted the old flier.

Sammy had already seen the Captain and parked his tractor against the sandbag wall. He climbed down.

"Anything more on the boy?" the Captain shouted.

Sammy shook his head. "Is Cathy's find a fishing lure like I figured?"

"Not fishing," said the Captain. "Look what I discovered." He reached into his jacket pocket and pulled out a plastic bag protecting the object. "Here, under the light."

The Captain went to stand under one of the large site spots. Pete and the others came over. As he held the item in the light, he pointed out black marks on the object.

"These scratches appear to me like a corroded part number."

"Part of what?" asked Sammy, spitting.

"Not sure when I started. The number might be a code used on aircraft parts so I checked around."

He opened his briefcase and pulled out a large bound book. "I came up with this." He opened the book to a page marked with a paper clip. "Boys, this is the parts schedule for a Republic P47 C Thunderbolt fighter aircraft, a model built in 1943 at Farmingdale, Long Island, New York." He pointed to the center of the page. "Here, this shows part of the rear-landing wheel."

Rain came down suddenly, drenching them. Hank managed to cover the book with his arm. They moved back closer to the light as the rain subsided.

"Rain makes me feel unwelcome," laughed the Captain.

"I guess you aren't," said Sammy.

The Captain went on, with Hank holding the book to the light. "Notice the casting for the tail wheel." He put the bagged item against the page. The metal object was similar.

"Allow for the corrosion, but I think it's part of the strut assembly. Been buried here for a long time."

"How long?"

"Don't jump to any conclusions. Zinnie Allingham was not the only one to crash a P47 in this swamp. I think more than five of them went in here."

Will said, "They found all the other ones. She did fly a Model C on her last flight."

"You're sure of all this?" asked Bob Johnny, from behind Will.

The Captain nodded. "Will's right. The other wrecks were all found. Over in the part of the swamp closest to the Bay."

"You think this is a wheel section, Captain?" asked Hank.

"Seen enough of them, for sure. In the war lot of times we had to help fix them, too. This thing broke off a P47. I even lost this strut on my own fighter when I bounced her tail in landing."

"Aunt Zinnie's plane," said Will. "Sure I'd find it. Sure."

"Don't get too excited, Will. This might still be a part fell off from those other wrecks," said the Captain.

"Yeah, but they were a couple of miles away from here, and the Army cleaned up all the wrecks," said Will.

The Captain continued, "I thought about those other lines in the earth."

"We're still finding them," said Hank.

"I think they're probably what's left of control cables. Parts were broken clear of the fuselage when she came in. Might be the individual strands unraveled and rusted in those curved patterns."

"Cables?" said Will.

"Seven strand cable controlling the rudder."

Will persisted, "So what can we do about this?"

"I been thinking. When I came home in 1945, I was out here one day and remember noticing the burial mound had lost a whole side of itself like a bulldozer had scraped dirt away. When I asked, some trappers told me the Easter storm in 1944 had brought in high water and washed soil away."

Pete nodded, considering. Hank recognized the look he had when he was deep in thought.

"Matter of fact," the Captain continued, "By the time I went to the mound a year had gone by and brush had built up." He stabbed at the muck with his shoe.

"Perhaps this fell 'cause of of one of these fighters training and passing overhead during the war," said Bob Johnny.

"Possible," agreed the Captain.

Sammy coughed and spit. "If a Thunderbolt fighter, a P47, heavy as those things were, cracked up coming in here, storm or no storm, people would know. What about the fire, the explosion?"

"I thought about that too," said the Captain. "The plane might have been caught by the storm in a downdraft bringing it straight down. If it were out of fuel, no fire would start. This swamp was water and muck even in those days. Whatever hole the crash made, would fill right back in and appear pretty much the same a few days later with the tide coming in and out. If the storm was a bad one, the wreck would be swallowed fast."

"I guess anything is possible," said Pete.

"I remember the wreck Will thought was his aunt's plane, the one found in the swamp outside Wilmington, Delaware," Sammy said. "We went with Will to see it."

Will smiled, "I thought she might have been wounded and confused about where she was."

"Anyway, that wreck proved the possibility of setting down in a swamp without damage to the airplane," said the Captain.

"Over in Delaware earth covered the wreck and pretty well preserved the metal," said Sammy.

"Well, I think the same kind of thing happened here," said the Captain. "If the pilot managed to set down easy and penetrate the soft mound, the fuselage could be sucked under the surface."

"I got no doubt anything heavy would eventually sink. A lot for soft mire to support," said Sammy.

"Five tons of aircraft," said the Captain. "The fighter could dig a pretty good-sized tunnel entrance. It might have gotten smaller over time. That could have been what Bobby found."

"You still paying on your reward, Will?" asked Pete.

Will stopped and stared at Pete, "You mean the reward for finding the P47? Sure, whoever finds her gets the reward."

"I still think any airplane would break into tiny pieces," said Sammy.

Captain Steele said, "My best guess says no. P47s were built too well."

"Your theory ain't helping us save this child," said Sammy, moving back to his tractor.

"Well, I sure got you interested, Will," said Captain Steele, grinning knowingly as he watched Will walking back and forth, the schoolteacher's eyes on the mound and the trench.

"Like Will asked, what do we do? We've already torn up a lot of the mound," said Bob Johnny.

"Will, you can bet Bob Johnny don't want to search for no plane," spit Sammy.

"He'll get in too much trouble with the politicians."

Will said, "All I'm saying is we ought to be thinking what we'll do if we do discover a plane sunk in here."

"Corroded and rusted," muttered Sammy, as he climbed up to the tractor seat.

"Might be a help in finding the boy," said the Captain. "Being out of the air, down under the ground, Sammy, rust won't be too bad. I'm even thinking that if there's some structure left of it, the boy might have found a refuge."

"So what do we do?" asked Sammy.

"We get the plane out," said Will.

"You're crazy," said Sammy.

"He may not be," said Captain Steele. "Remember, Republic built tough aircraft. The Nazi pilots found that out."

"What about Bobby?" Hank asked, picking up a shovel.

"Maybe Bobby is inside it like you say. Get Bobby out first, of course," said Will.

"You're damn right," said Melissa, coming over from the radio tent where she had been helping Charlie.

Hank walked away to return to his digging. He left the decisions on the mound to Sammy.

Betty followed Hank over to the trench. "You think my brother isn't interested in Bobby," she said.

"Your brother is being your brother like he always does."

"Aunt Zinnie's estate and her last will and testament, Hank, drives him."

"What do you mean?"

"She wrote one."

"Didn't your brother inherit the school from his father?" asked Hank, chopping at the wall.

"Yes," said Betty. "The swamp was mentioned, too. Will and I don't own the swamp. We can rent space like he does for his hunting business, but we can't sell it for development."

"Folks say you guys have to wait for some years to get the rights to sell."

"Zinnie owned this land. Her last will and testament stated her body had to buried on her land, this island, so to speak. Otherwise after a certain time the swamp was to be sold to the state for an animal preserve."

"Her body was never found so the land goes to the state and Will loses out," said Hank.

"The estate is to be settled this year," Betty said. "Will is frantic. We'll lose a lot of money selling to the government."

"You never seemed to bother about your family inheritance."

"Hank," she smiled, "You know I'm not a big shot. I'm glad the swamp goes for a preserve. Everything but the burial mound of Jimmy's Nanticoke tribe is our property and covered by Zinnie's will. Will wants to get title to all the swamp, fill parts with topsoil, and then build expensive condominiums. He'd make a lot of money doing that and he dreams of being rich like our parents and grandparents were."

"I care about getting my boy back, Betty. If Will wants to help, fine. Otherwise he should stay the hell away from me."

She nodded. "Finding this airplane here means he might find Zinnie's body. She'd be buried in the Wilderness to meet the will requirements. I know his mind. I try to understand him."

Hank returned to digging, trying to match the other men as they worked in precision against the tractor's travels, back and forth. He had his strength back. Far down in the direction of the boat ramp and along the walkway, behind the sandbags, the children climbed the side of the mound. Hank was worried about the girl's safety and started to wave Cathy down.

"Come here," she called. Richard was with her.

Hank motioned to Pete. Cathy and Richard were in the middle of the mound, near the open field where the workers were filling sandbags. They were squatting down at a place more than halfway across, their weight supported by the small squares of plywood strapped to their shoes. Cathy's face was close to the earth among some low bushes and vines, motionless if she had spotted something.

"What, Cathy?" Hank called.

"He went down into this cut."

"Who?" asked Pete.

"Cochise."

Hank shrugged his shoulders and started back to the trench.

"No, wait. I want to explain," she called after him.

He turned his head toward Cathy again.

"I think he's with Bobby," said Cathy.

"She's got a point," said Pete. "The hole might go down near where Bobby is. Bobby said he felt fresh air before the cave collapsed. Breeze may have come in to a den." Pete stood back and measured with his eyes from the trench to the hole where the children were squatting.

"The mound's two hundred feet around. Cathy's hole is near the center. He'd have to crawl more than a hundred feet to get there," Pete finally said.

"I got an idea," said Richard.

The adults turned their heads towards the black child.

Cathy explained, "Richard can do electronics."

Richard said, "Charlie and me could send down something to Bobby."

"Rig a line down, something with a speaker and a mike," said Charlie, nodding at Richard.

"If Bobby is getting air, we'd have to be sure not to wreck the hole," said Pete. He waved to Sammy, who stopped the tractor and climbed down.

"Do something as fast as you can," Sammy said.

Charlie, who was at his radio a hundred feet away, took off his earphones as the storm rain drizzled around him. "Richard, you come over and give me a hand in this mud. Yessir. Got to get the line to go straight down."

"Remember, we ain't got much time left," said Sammy, staring out at the rising tidewater and heading to the tractor.

Richard said, "We can put some weight on the mike and speaker to make them drop faster. We'd hear on the microphone and talk on the speaker."

"I don't know," said Charlie. "We can do the electronics. We just can't be sure whether the stuff will drop." Charlie, on a canvas chair, was more than two times the size of Richard, who stood in front of him in the tent, his head barely up to the dials of the radio.

"I want to listen," said Melissa. "Make sure to attach the radio receiver to some loudspeakers."

Charlie glanced at the hole. "Let's say we are ten to twenty feet over the level of where Bobby might be," he said. "At an angled hole path the mike might have to go thirty feet. If the hole drops good without any rough spots to hang-up, so much the better."

"We're hoping," said Pete, tall over the others.

"Did you understand Captain Steele, Melissa?" asked Will.

She turned to him, "You mean about Zinnie's airplane being down under the mound?"

"Yes. What do you think?"

"Will, we're all more concerned about my son."

"We got to get some more equipment up here, Melissa."

"What effort that we are not already doing?" she asked, listening.

"Order a dredge to dig quickly," said Will.

Pete said, "Even if we used more equipment in this storm, I figure it's too much risk to the boy. Even the tractor we have might make the whole thing collapse on him."

She asked Hank, "Do you think we need anything more to help Bobby? I'd pay for it."

"Ask her for a dredge, Hank, something with a suction device, to pull the muck out," said Will. "No danger to the boy."

"You don't want to help Bobby," said Hank. "You want to dig an airplane."

Will appealed to Melissa, "He's not being fair, Melissa. After all, the airplane might be lost forever when this tide gets in. The trench is too slow."

"I guess what people say is true. You are pitiful. I deserve you," she said, walking away.

Richard left Charlie who was finishing up the electronic package material. The boy stood next to Hank, his head barely to Hank's shoulder.

"I want to find my friend, Bobby," he said.

"I understand," Hank said, putting his arm around the boy.

"My dad say I can stay here until you say."

"You spend a lot of time with your dad, don't you?"

"We go out buddy on his twin cylinder BMW."

"You're lucky he takes you on his motorcycle."

"Bobby says he likes being with you," said Richard.

"I like him too," said Hank.

"He didn't want his grandfather's letter."

"Did he tell you why?"

"He said that his grandfather was different in the letter and he lied."

Hank asked, surprised. "Did he say what he lied about?"

"Nossir." Richard went on, "My father and me, this summer we are going to ride to Canada. His family lives in Montreal."

"Montreal?" asked Hank.

"My daddy, he's a US citizen but he came from Nigeria when he was my age. He is a chief in his tribe in Nigeria." He paused.

"You are the chief's son. You'll go someday to visit your African family."

"Like Cochise."

"How's that?" asked Hank.

"He's the chief's son, too. He's the son of Sachem." Richard continued, "Cochise is trying to talk to us. Cathy thinks so, too."

Hank helped Richard get back up the side of the mound.

"You and Cathy can help Charlie with the speaker," he said as he started to walk back to his work in the trench.

Hank's feet were sunk in several inches of swirling black liquid, bits of reed and clusters of unearthed roots floating in the eddy. He realized the time for a chance of rescue of his son was almost gone. Tears began coming down his cheeks, their warmth mixing with the constant rain pelting his skin.

Chapter Eleven

"OK," said Charlie, standing up. "This setup works as well as it's going to work. Let's get started."

He signaled Cathy to come near from her perch at the muskrat hole. Charlie had set up the base two-meter transceiver - what had been the regular fire department radio set. He attached a speaker and microphone to the end of a transmitter wire and taped the two together so they would fall through the hole at the same time.

She asked, "OK, Charlie, what do you want me to do?"

He handed her the taped unit and a coil of thin wire. "You weigh less than me. It wouldn't be smart for me to sit on the plywood. I'd sink the whole project. You're going to have to do this, Cathy. You and Richard. I want you two to lower this carefully down that hole. When it stops moving, just jiggle it some and see if it won't keep on going. If it stops completely, don't force anything. Keep calling out your progress."

Will did not say anything or try to prevent his daughter crawling out on the mound. He was obviously preoccupied with figuring a way to dredge out the aircraft.

Pete, however, sensed that the children were in some danger. He could see that Melissa was also concerned about risking Richard as well as Will's daughter in the muck.

"They'll do all right," he said to her.

"What happens if those devices get into water?" asked Will, suddenly aware of what was going on.

"Well, maybe the tape will keep them waterproof and maybe it won't. We'll see," said Charlie. "Don't go too fast, Cathy," he called, his voice breaking in the sudden wind. He and the Captain kept slack in the cable from the tent. From the loudspeakers came the noise of scraping as the microphone slipped further into the ground and brushed the sides of the muskrat tunnel.

"We're down maybe two feet," reported Cathy.

"You can start broadcasting on that speaker, Captain Steele," said Charlie.

The captain picked up the microphone. "Bobby, Bobby, Bobby. This is Captain Steele and the River Sunday Fire Department. Can you hear me?"

They heard only the noise of the wind in reply. The loudspeakers blared as they continued to produce intermittent sounds of metal against earth, the noises jarring. Each time the listeners looked up expectantly at the speakers clamped high on the light poles, each of them thinking that this might be Bobby's first answer. Each sound was another disappointment; however, proving to be only static as Charlie shook his head to confirm that the noise meant nothing.

To Hank, each noise resembled a heartbeat. He thought about Bobby breathing, his heart pounding.

He shivered as he remembered feeling his own heartbeat in the war. His war was fighting the enemy infiltrators at the perimeter of an airbase. He never knew if he killed anyone, only that he fired and was fired at, great numbers of rounds flying in the night raids.

Maybe Bobby would be lucky like he was. Maybe his life would also be spared. An Air Force colonel, who was one of those in charge of the facility, found out that Hank knew about gardens. Hank was brought into the next room where the colonel, a short man, sat in a metal chair. His head moved quickly from Hank's face to different piles of papers and back again to Hank's face. They exchanged salutes and he asked Hank to sit down, at ease.

The colonel appraised him for a few moments without speaking, still shuffling some papers on his desk.

"Private, I understand you're a gardener."

"Yes, Sir."

"Are you any good?"

"Yes, Sir," Hank said.

"I like to have my bases orderly, pretty. We have visitors, sometimes from Washington. They want to see a place like home," the colonel said.

"Yes, Sir."

The colonel turned up his face to Hank, "Have you seen the flowers here around the buildings?"

"Yes, Sir."

"What do you think?"

"We got a need for more color spread, Sir. Move some of them around, that's all."

The colonel smiled. "I want you to take charge, be my gardener, do that."

"I can try, Sir."

"I'm going to borrow you from your outfit. You'll stand guard when your company officers need you for fighting in this Goddamn war, but otherwise I want you working on my flowers."

"Yes, Sir."

"Maybe we'll both get out of here alive," he said. "That's all, Private."

"Yes, Sir."

That was his reprieve. Hank spent most of his tour planting flowers.

Hank had arranged plants to show the flags of the allied countries side by side with the colors of the flowers. He had a Republic of Vietnam flag in yellow and red and of course the Stars and Stripes in red, white, and blue. Other flags of the Australians and Koreans were also there. Some of the flowers he had to use had large petals and the configuration of the plants was difficult especially in regulating heights. His Vietnamese workers were helpful in changing the plants around to make the display attractive. The Washington visitors were very impressed and left for dinner with the colonel after congratulating Hank for his work. The Vietnamese workers were also lined up and each was given a handshake by an official. The colonel of course stood in the background and said from time to time that this was a fine example of Vietnamese and American cooperation.

At the presentation one Vietnamese woman, unannounced, proceeded to the back of the garden plot and inserted a small white crucifix into the earth.

Mudman, however, was assigned the task of going into a tunnel complex along with two other American soldiers. Within ten minutes both of the other men were shot dead from ahead. He wanted to turn back but on the radio his officer ordered him to continue. The tunnel was dark. He told Hank that he smelled this strange perfume. He had no way to use any light because the beam might draw fire. He couldn't use a grenade because the explosion might collapse the tunnel on him. He had to keep crawling forward, hoping he could find the enemy before the enemy found him. After a few more minutes he entered a small tunnel to the side of the main tunnel. He stopped and listened. The perfume grew stronger.

He had told Hank that he heard a click. He suspected it was a rifle bolt closing. He wasn't wrong. Rounds went by him, flashing but not making enough light so he could see ahead in the tunnel. He immediately shot into the darkness, the flashes from his bullets skipping over the walls, ricocheting back and forth. When his rifle magazine was empty, he reloaded and emptied a second magazine. After that was empty, he waited in the silence. He still smelled the perfume. After a few more minutes, he moved ahead.

In the dark, he began to crawl over arms and legs of human bodies, wet and still warm. He turned on his flashlight after he placed it aiming away and several feet from him, in case he had to draw fire to it. No return fire came. The angle of the light revealed the collapsed bodies of several women, a young man and some boys and girls. Guns and grenades were in the hands of the each of the dead and he knew that he would have been dead if he had not fired and killed them. The light displayed a cave room with a small wooden platform decorated with Viet Cong flags. On the ground was a tiny set of plastic figures including one stretched on a wooden crucifix. On a folding table were the remains of several plates of rice and a bottle of water. All over the dirt floor were scattered hundreds of blossoms, great aromatic blooms of local flowers. Mudman said it looked like Ho Chi Minh on the cross and some kind of religious symbolic supper. Also, written with paint on the wall were the English words of Bob Dylan's song about blowing in the wind.

"Bobby, this is Captain Steele."

Hank heard Captain Steele repeating his message. Beside him, Charlie, with his earphones clipped under his fire helmet, twisted and adjusted dials of the transceiver alert for any possible sound that might be human. At the side of the tent, their faces glaring from the work light and the glimmer from the radio dials were Melissa and Will, stern-faced and attentive. Also Pete stood with them, taller, his eyes alert. Sammy came and went from his tractor always supervising the trench and wall construction, and coughing from time to time. Bob Johnny and the reporters stood at the edge, behind the others, like strangers at a party who were not really welcome. The two children were at the hole in the center of the mound, holding the wire. Betty, in turn, stood near him.

It was an eerie moment, this attention by all of them to the speakers. Hank found himself like his former wife, and Pete and Sammy, mouthing the Captain's messages as they were repeated, saying them to themselves like a common prayer, like a chant, that the words would be heard by Bobby. As the minutes went by and the rain continued to come down harder and harder, Hank hoped that soon the speakers would broadcast the first sound of hope, not some click of death.

Chapter Twelve

A sound, a thump as of a fist against a wooden table top, smashed over the speaker, then repeated. The noises came through at random intervals, sometimes every minute then only every two or three minutes, but louder over the ensuing minutes as the microphone descended inch by inch, the speaker giving out much static and scraping noises.

Charlie called up to Cathy, "That's like what I heard before. How far down are we?"

"About fifteen feet of wire," she replied.

"Can you bring them in better?" asked Captain Steele.

"I'm trying." Charlie nodded and shifted another of his switches with no improvement.

"Sammy, shut her down," the Captain called out. The tractor sound stopped and the firemen working with shovels were suddenly quiet. Everyone waited and listened to the thumping sounds.

"It must be human. No animal could make that noise. He's alive, Hank," said the Captain leaning out of the tent. He reached over Charlie's shoulder and adjusted another dial. "This might help," he said.

Charlie shook his head. "That will make it worse." He moved the switch back to where it had been set.

The Captain picked up the microphone and broadcast again. "Bobby, Bobby, Bobby. Do you hear us? This is Captain Steele. Speak out. We got a transmitter down there with you. We'll hear you. Speak out as loud as you can."

The thumps suddenly stopped.

"Bobby, Bobby, Bobby, answer me back. This is Captain Steele. We're all here to rescue you."

They heard a garble of sounds that could have be Bobby's voice. The noises were weak, perhaps the chatter of a family of muskrats or perhaps, as Hank hoped, jumbled words saying, strangely, over and over, "Get back, and get back."

Following the so-called words, they heard another thump. Then the Captain stood up and walked out into the rain, carrying his microphone. He stood by the edge of the mound, looking at Cathy and Richard on their perch out on the top of the mound.

"Bobby, we hear you. It's all right, Bobby," his steady voice repeated slowly.

Hank wanted to jump up on the mound and tear at the hole in the earth to free his child. He was halfway up the side of the muddy slope when the Captain grabbed his shoulder.

"That won't work, Hank." The Captain continued, "I'd like to go out there and start digging myself. We all know better. The surface is too soft. That's why the kids are the only ones we can have out there. Any more weight and the whole thing could collapse."

The Captain said, slowly, with more emotion than usual, "Give us a chance to do this right."

"What do you make of it?" Hank asked.

"I know that was him we heard. I'm just not sure he heard us," said Charlie. "That microphone has gone over a few bumps."

"Can you lower it more, Cathy?" the Captain called.

"Yes," she answered.

Charlie had tension on the end of the line to keep it taut. "Give her and Richard slack to let it down more," the Captain ordered him. Charlie reached over and loosened the reel of wire beside his table.

Cathy yelled, "Hey. The line slipped down a couple of feet more. It just dropped down."

She left Richard controlling the line and crawled back to Charlie's side. "Let me try," she said as she took the microphone from the Captain. "Bobby, it's me."

For a moment or so there was silence, except for some background static. Then Hank heard sobs mixed with the sounds of gasping for breath, and Bobby's first distinct word to them came over the speakers.

"Cathy," a voice said. It sounded like Bobby, but weak and distorted.

The voice paused, then spoke again, this time louder, "Cathy. Help me. It's so dark." The voice stopped and they heard only the slight crackling noise.

"Bobby," she said. Her hand was trembling.

Bobby, his voice this time clear and full and recognizable, replied, "Cathy, you got out OK. What about Richard?"

"We're all right, Bobby. Here's Captain Steele." She handed the microphone back, almost dropping it she was so excited.

"I'm cold, Captain Steele," said Bobby. "I want to get out."

"Bobby, this is Captain Steele. We're all here, your mother and father and the firemen. We're going to get you out as soon as we can."

"Don't leave me."

"Just keep on being brave. We won't leave you, Bobby."

"It must be raining," said Bobby. "I keep hearing the sound of water dripping."

"How far away?" asked the Captain?

"At least ten feet. I'm standing on something so I don't fall in the water."

"Tell me what you are standing on, Bobby?" continued the Captain.

Bobby started crying. They listened to his sobbing. The Captain waved to Sammy and the tractor started up again. Hank thought the speed of the men's shoveling was faster.

Bobby spoke again, "When the cave fell in, there was no more light. I felt my way along. On my right, the hole got bigger for a little while. I gave up calling."

"Your friends went for help, Bobby."

"I didn't hear anybody. The hole behind me started to fill up so I figured the best thing was kept moving ahead to where the air was. I crawled a long way."

Static interrupted the words. Charlie fiddled with the radio knobs and it cleared.

"Tell me where you hear the speaker," said the Captain.

"Your voice is coming from my right side. I can't reach the radio but I think I know where it is. I don't want to move too much."

"That's all right. You just keep talking from where you are."

"I started to crawl out of the caved in section. The roof was very wet and I was afraid that it might come down. I couldn't see anything, but I could feel the walls of the passage coming closer together and I knew I was going down deeper. I felt fresh air on my face. I hoped for a while I could find a way out. On my left the wall got real smooth and curved in, smoother than the wall on the right. I thought it might be metal, because it was cold compared to the soil. I came to a place where I was crawling on what felt like a lot of roots. The passage got more level, not going up but just level."

When he had controlled his sobs, he said, "It smells bad here, like a toilet that has been plugged up for a long time."

Bobby went on, "Then my knees were on top of what I thought was a large round cylinder. I figured it was a big root, maybe of an old tree. I also thought it might be some Native American stuff, like a mummy or something. I got even more scared."

The Captain turned to Hank and Pete and covered the microphone. "If this is a P47 in there, that's probably part of the plane's high altitude supercharger that he is describing. I think he's up in the fuselage."

Will bent closer.

Bobby's young voice continued from the speaker, "In the dark I felt a lot of space around me. My face brushed against roots hanging in the air."

Bobby forced himself to swallow a sob. "Then I found a flat area like a shelf and climbed up on it. That's where I am."

"Tell me about the flat area," asked the Captain.

"Lots of bones here. I don't like sitting next to them." Bobby paused again. "It stinks. This place has lots of animals living here. One of them just jumped on me. I hit at it several times with my shoe but I know it's still there in the dark."

"What else is around you, Bobby?"

"Under the flat place I think I feel shoes or boots with bones coming out of them."

Sammy said, "The trench is still the closest to Bobby. I figure the boy's location is about fifty or less feet from the end of our trench, closer than coming in from the sides or the other end of the mound."

The Captain said, "I agree. We keep going the way we are. If we come in from any other way, we might disturb the mound more."

The loudspeakers boomed out Bobby's voice, "I can't keep the animals away much longer."

Pete said, "Let's try to send down a flashlight to him. He can keep the animals back with the light."

The Captain said, "Bobby, the passage you came in, what condition is it?"

The child's voice said. "It's filled with muck and water."

"That's what I figured," Captain Steele nodded as he covered the mike again. "That will be our job, to dig that passage out again, the way he went in."

He smiled at Cathy. "Good work on reaching Bobby. You must have talked on a radio before," he said.

She grinned. Hank, like most people in town, knew she and the Captain had a secret, that she was taking flying lessons from him, lessons that her father, Will, would have forbidden if he had known. She took figure skating lessons as her father wanted, then sneaked to the airfield a mile away and flew, returning to the rink just in time for her father to see her perform her jumps. Cathy Ellingham's flying lessons were a River Sunday cover-up that many, including Hank and Bobby, helped maintain.

"Bobby, can you still hear me?" asked the Captain.

"Yes, Captain Steele."

"Good. We're going to send down a light. I want you to describe more about the area where you are."

"It's a big space. I could stand up if I needed to. I'm afraid though. The platform is weak. When I push some of it too hard, my fingers just press through because it's rotten."

"No, don't stand up. Just feel around you. In front of you is there a lever sticking up from the floor?"

Bobby was silent for a few minutes. Then he said, "I found it. Yes, there is a lever straight up. How did you know that?"

"We think you are inside an airplane fuselage, Bobby."

"An airplane? Down here?"

"Everything points that way, as strange as it seems."

"I might have figured that out too, if I could have had some light." He paused. "Maybe I've found Zinnie's plane," he said.

A noise, like scraping metal, came over the speakers.

Then they heard Bobby scream.

"What happened?"

"The whole thing shifted under me. It keeps moving forward, a little at a time," he said, his voice shaking.

"Is your foot all right?"

"I think so. I stepped into the muskrats. I could feel them moving around my foot."

He screamed again, and then sobbed, "Oh, get me out of here. Get me out of here. Please get me out of here."

Melissa tugged at Captain Steele's arm. "Stop all these damn questions. You're going to get him killed. Now see what you have done?"

"We have to know all we can," said Captain Steele patiently.

Pete put his arm around Melissa. "The Captain's right. We need to know. This airplane frame, if that's what it is, will help keep the mud from falling in."

The screams subsided.

The Captain tried again, "Bobby, are you all right?"

Bobby had stopped sobbing. They heard sounds of Bobby's hard breathing.

"There. I'm back up on the platform," he said. "When I was near that lever I felt something else."

"What?"

"I felt what might be the instrument panel of the plane."

"Now, listen to me. Don't touch that instrument panel again," said the Captain.

"Why?"

"Some of those instruments were made with radium. The stuff is radioactive. It will hurt you. Just stay back on your seat."

"Lots of animals in here," Bobby's voice was getting nervous again, "It's like a giant nest of animals."

"Melissa, maybe you can calm him down," said the Captain, offering her the microphone.

Melissa was unsteady as she walked toward the Captain. Hank thought she might still be drunk from her Easter party, but then he realized that she was walking hesitantly because she was scared.

"What should I say," she whispered to Hank, before she took the mike.

"You'll do fine," Hank said, his hand touching hers.

Melissa grimaced and took the microphone. She stared at it for almost a minute then began to talk to Bobby. At first her voice was low, barely audible in the speakers, as she gathered confidence.

"I love you, Bobby."

"I love you too, Mommy."

Hank heard her pause her normally cocky voice, as if she were searching for something positive, something reassuring, to say to their son. She needed something to cover up the trembling and stop the tears in her eyes.

"Your birthday party is all set for next Saturday night," she said.

The child's voice came back, calm and steady. "I know. All the kids are coming."

While she was speaking to Bobby, the Captain and Charlie were devising an apparatus to slide a flashlight down the radio wire.

"Test it again. Turn it on," said the Captain and as Charlie did, the small beam lit up their intense faces.

"Last thing we want is for that light to get all the way down there and then not work. We'll lower it with the beam turned on."

"Yes," Melissa was talking to her son. "I've arranged for the man you like from the radio station to come and play tapes."

"You can come too, Mommy."

"I hope you will dance with me," she said.

"Did you ever dance with your father?" he asked.

"I used to dance with the General. My father was always away in sailing races and regattas."

"I wish the General was still alive so he could come."

"He'd be proud of you. I miss him too, every day. He saw you when you were a baby but you don't remember that."

"I don't remember the General. I remember seeing you and Daddy, that's all."

Bobby moved and they could hear the creaking of the structure he was inside.

"Did you like my other grandfather?"

"Of course I did," said Melissa.

"You never told me so," Bobby said.

"Both grandfathers were friends," said Melissa.

"Kids told me your father was not brave," said Bobby.

"Your Dad's father told me something about my dad. He sat down with me on the porch one night when we were still living at the garden store and he told me."

"What did he say?" asked Bobby. "I want to know now, Mommy."

Melissa glanced around her at the firemen, their faces rapt as they listened to the speaker. Then she whispered into the microphone. "He said that he would have surrendered the boat, too. He said that the lives of the men were more important."

"Why didn't the people in town agree?"

"I don't know, Bobby. He was a very wise man and knew a lot about things besides gardens."

"As much as the General?"

"In his own way, yes, he did," she said. She was quiet, and then changed the subject. "You have lots of presents already waiting for you at home."

"I know. I saw the pile in your bedroom."

She laughed. "You're a little spy, Bobby."

"Are Pete and Chief Sammy up there too?"

"Sure. Mister Allingham is here, too. He has a present for your birthday."

"I don't want to talk to him."

Melissa moved her face back slightly from the microphone as if she didn't know what to reply. Bobby went on, "I want to talk to Daddy. Can Daddy come to my party this year?"

"I'll ask him." Melissa gave the microphone to Charlie and walked over to the edge of the mound where Hank was helping with the flashlight.

"He wants to talk to you," she said to Hank.

Hank helped to pass the flashlight and its clip along the wire. It reached Cathy and she and Richard started it going into the hole.

"Let it drop along the other wire," said Charlie.

"It's moving down," said Cathy. "I can feel it sinking."

Will Allingham picked up the microphone. "Bobby, it's Mister Allingham."

Pete said to Hank, "Will's pretty formal with the kid, isn't he?"

"He's the schoolmaster."

"He's going to be Bobby's stepfather?"

"He tries, I guess," said Hank.

Will asked, "How are you doing, Bobby?"

"All right, sir."

"Listen to me, Bobby. Do you remember when we talked about my aunt, Zinnie Allingham, at school?"

"Sure."

"Well, you know how we all been searching for that airplane of hers."

"Yessir. This might be her wrecked fighter plane."

"I know." Will stared at the ground as he clutched the microphone tightly. "You said there were boots and bones in there with you. Can you tell me more about them?"

"It's kinda scary."

"Well, feel around you there and if you come up with anything, let me know. It might help to identify the airplane."

"Do I get the reward?"

"If you have found my aunt's airplane, then you get the reward."

"Course I want to share it with Cathy and Richard. They helped, too."

"All right."

"One thing I found," said Bobby.

"What is that?"

"I was going to surprise Mommy with it when I get out of here."

"What is it, son?" asked Will.

"It feels like a ring."

"Where did you find it?" Will asked, his voice faster in pace.

"It was on the platform just as I climbed up on it. Lots of little bones near it. It was in the pile of those bones."

"My aunt had a ring on her finger when she was lost. Tell me about it." Will was trembling with excitement. Hank heard it in the man's voice.

"Sure, Mister Allingham. I put the ring in my pocket. Let me pull it out."

Hank moved back to the radio. He stood next to Melissa and touched Will on the shoulder. Will turned and saw Melissa and Hank together. "Just asking him a little bit about the place he is in," said Will, pulling back.

"You leave him alone," said Hank.

Melissa grabbed at Hank's arm. Hank immediately got her message he should not start a fight. She was afraid her child would hear the argument over the microphone still tightly clenched in Will's fist.

The child's voice crackled on the speaker. "Here it is. Let me try to feel it." Then silence. "Wait a minute, Sir."

"What happened?" asked Will.

Hank's hand tightened on Will's shoulder.

"I dropped it. It's in the water at my feet."

"Can you reach it?" asked Will, his voice rising.

Hank whispered, "Leave him alone, Will. I'm warning you."

Bobby called up, "No, I can't find it. The water is too deep."

The child began to whimper. "Wait a minute, Mister Allingham. Let me try again. I really want the reward. I just have trouble keeping my balance on this old piece of metal. Maybe it has fallen below to where the muskrats have their nest. They are making more noises now."

"You can do it, boy. It's important," persisted Will, his eyes wide in anticipation.

Melissa's voice was high. "It's not important!"

The Captain forcibly took the microphone. "Bobby," he said, "Forget about that ring. We're sending down a flashlight. You should be able to see the light pretty soon. You can use the light to scare away the animals."

Bobby whimpered. "I also found a necklace hanging in front of me. When I touched it, the jewels fell into to the water. Part of it felt like a crucifix. I'm sorry."

Will moved to the side, staring at the microphone, his face showing astonishment, his eyes still intent. "She took an ivory rosary with her when she flew in those airplanes."

"It might be her rosary and it might not be," said Hank.

"I don't see the light yet," said Bobby. "Wait a minute. I see a glow to my right."

They waited at the edge of the mound in the rain and wind gusts, listening for Bobby's next words. The water from outside the sandbags had continued to leak and was covering Hank's shoes up to his ankles.

Chapter Thirteen

"It's like weak candle light," said Bobby. "I think the animals are playing with the light because it's moving back and forth sending shadows all around me."

Bobby's voice grew stronger. The light seemed to have given him courage. "The flashlight is near me behind some metal and I can't reach it. The muskrats are quiet. They usually do a lot of scratching so I know they are worried about it. They are smart animals though and it may not be long before they will break it, maybe chew the wire."

"Tell us what you see around you," said the Captain.

"I'm inside an airplane all right. Over top of me, way up too far for me to reach is the top of the cockpit. Outside to my left is earth packed tight against the glass but to the right I see a space where the light is coming from. Glass or plastic because of the way it reflects the light. It has metal running along the glass, like a greenhouse."

"That's the canopy all right, one of the older P47 models, what they called the razorbacks," grinned the Captain to Hank, away from the microphone. Then, into the mike, "Keep going, Bobby. You're doing fine."

The Captain studied his manual. He traced a schematic with his finger as he spoke. "Bobby must have entered the fuselage from near the tail on the left side. We must have sent the light and mike down on the airplane's front right, her starboard side, up along the engine and canopy. That would be right here," he pointed to a top view of a P47. The Captain spoke into the mike, "What's in front of you?"

"It's definitely the instrument panel. Of course, it's all chewed up and there's instruments hanging out on their wires. I see the turn and bank indicator. It's glowing a little in the light. I'll stay away from it, like you said. The control stick is right in front of me."

Static began on the loudspeakers.

"How fast is the water coming in, Bobby?"

"It must be my aunt's plane," said Will, interrupting.

"We're all aware what you're interested in, Will," Hank said.

Bobby went on, "I can't say for sure. Now that I have some light, I'll watch the height of the water against the wall. I'm on the edge of a metal seat. Bones of a skeleton are on my right side stretched up against the canopy. It seems to be a person. The person's flying suit is holding together most of the skeleton except the skull which must have fallen into the water. I see a stain on the cloth of the suit."

"Ask him if it's a man or woman," said Will.

The Captain ignored him.

Bobby went on, "Seems like the person was trying to get out. I see scraping marks on the canopy top. The pilot must have got caught down here and couldn't get out. Maybe wounded." More static came through, louder.

"Am I going to get caught down here, too?" Hank could hear sobs. He knew Bobby was losing what little confidence he had.

"I got a cut on my knee and the blood has dried," Bobby said. "That must have been what was attracting the muskrats. I see their eyes all around me in the corners."

"Bobby, I know it's hard for you, real hard, but you have to wait a little longer."

The Captain clicked off the microphone.

Hank said, "I still think we should just go for him, go down directly to him."

"We've been over this," said the Captain. "The top of the mound would collapse on him. With all that soil coming down on him, he wouldn't have a chance. Besides, he's already said the plane was moving. If we cause any more pressure, especially by digging on top of it, the plane might go on into the muck and we'll never get him."

"The Captain's right," said Sammy. "Getting a light down there is one thing, but digging a hole might shift the wreck. That wreck, it's like a teeter-totter, barely balanced. We're better doing what we're doing."

Pete said, "When we get to the tail, and I don't know how much longer that will be, Captain Steele, but I'm sure it will be soon, then maybe we can secure it with lines so the plane won't slip any more."

"Good," said the Captain. "Once we have a hold on it then we can figure what to do. Could be we're close enough to just come quick along the left side of the fuselage to get to him"

"While we're doing that, we've got to keep Bobby from losing hope," said Hank.

"I wish I could touch him; comfort him," said Melissa.

The Captain turned on the microphone and spoke to Bobby. "Richard's here to talk to you."

"Sure," Bobby said.

Richard had been Bobby's best friend for more than a year. Richard's father was brought to River Sunday by the conglomerate that bought the Chesapeake Hotel. Most people assumed he, being a black man, had been sent to stop the workers, also mostly black, from forming a union and putting the hotel out of business with higher costs. The outcome of his mission was not yet known. Meanwhile, Richard was one of the most popular kids at the Allingham School. Besides his sense of humor and his stories about living in the city, he was the school expert on the latest computer games.

Richard clambered down from the top of the mound where he had been helping Cathy. He took the microphone, held it in front of his face, and said, "Hey, man."

"Richard."

"You got to hang on, Bobby. You and me, we been in this kind of fix before, you remember?"

"At your father's hotel?"

"Smelly shoes," said Richard. They had been in an empty room when a man and woman entered. They hid under the bed while the adults were above them.

"Her's were worse," said Bobby.

The laughter sounded like choking on the loudspeakers.

"Did you tell your Dad?" asked Bobby.

"No," said Richard. "Forever. He would have taken away my computer forever."

"Richard, tell my dad to hurry up. The light keeps going out."

Richard said, "I got the new cheat codes."

"Did you get through the magic wall?"

"They work. I can't wait to show you."

"What happens?"

"You see this valley and you have to cross it in a balloon."

At the other end of the mound, Hank heard Sammy stop the tractor. The silence made the swamp seem almost at peace. A tall woman running a high-sided white outboard, its rumble getting louder, was working in close to shore.

Pete said, "Birdey Pond."

"She doesn't like Sammy," said Hank. Pond and her associates had put negative advertisements in Duke's newspaper about Sammy's service station. The building and pumps had been located on the same corner in River Sunday since automobiles were invented and his grandfather had put in gasoline tanks to service them. The tanks bothered her and the others; they claimed leakage was fouling the town water supply. No end of tests by Sammy had satisfied her and nothing short of taking down the station and pulling the tanks out of the ground, would, as Sammy told Hank, ever satisfy her.

Rain bent the sides of her plastic rain hat. In the trench, the firemen who had been digging stopped, almost at attention. Sammy leaned over his steering wheel, silently staring at the boat and its driver

"You never can figure what that woman is thinking," said Pete.

The boat was close to shore and Hank could see the animals riding. Several raccoons were perched on the forward deck like point scouts and in the stern there were a number of muskrats. Their small heads, bobbing beside the white fiberglass of the boat resembled a miniature team of commandoes, ready to storm the mound. Yet he knew these were the bedraggled survivors of the high water, water that had probably already washed out several dens of these creatures and likely killed their babies.

Bob Johnny carried his shovel as he walked to the edge of the water and stood on the sandbag wall. He was not more than twenty feet from the boat as Missus Pond cruised by, still not speaking, just staring at the rescue workers.

Bob Johnny lifted his right arm and waved. She waved back, then turned her eyes ahead and sped off, finished what seemed to be her recon of the rescue status. In a few moments she was out of sight in the rain and darkness.

Richard motioned to Hank to take the microphone.

"He wants to talk to me," Hank said to Melissa. She was sitting on a canvas stool that Charlie had rigged for her and she moved her head upward to see him. Her eyes showed him some of the respect, the love they had for each other many years ago, before he went to war, before their teamwork failed.

"Bobby loves you," she said.

"Yes."

"I guess he's needed both of us for a long time."

He held the mike in both of his hands for a moment.

"You're cold," he said to her.

She pulled back and said, "I'll be all right."

He shook as Melissa had when she knew her time had come to speak to the boy. He lifted the microphone and, forcing himself to speak above a whisper, as if fearing the noise would further harm his son, said slowly and carefully, "Bobby, it's Daddy."

Chapter Fourteen

Hank said. "I'd take your place if I could."

"Dad, no way. You couldn't stand it down here."

"I just don't like to think of you there."

"I bet I know more about claustrophobia than you do," said Bobby. "Richard and I researched it on his computer."

Hank smiled, remembering his son was smarter than he was, a better student, talent Bobby inherited from his grandfather. "What did you guys find out?"

"The doctors would put you down here like I am. They say if they flood you with being closed in, they can cure you."

"Flood?" said Hank, thinking of water.

"The shrinks call it flooding. You'd be really messed up."

"Flooding," Hank repeated.

Bobby said, "I'm sorry I ran out of the store."

"That's all right."

"You know why I came here, Dad?"

"I would have told you nothing was worth climbing around in a cave in this kind of weather."

"I didn't count on the accident."

"We can talk about it later," Hank replied.

Bobby went on, "I'm sorry I've caused so much trouble." He paused then said, "Daddy, if I get out of here, will you still get me the signature of Harold Baines?"

"Next time he comes to town," Hank smiled. Baines was a baseball hero, a current one still in the Big Leagues, whose family lived near River Sunday.

"So you forgive me?"

"Sure."

"I miss Grandfather watching my games," said Bobby. "Did he go to your games?"

"Yes."

"He was never very good," said Bobby

"No, baseball wasn't my father's sport."

Bobby said, "I like your daffodils more than ever. I think I like them better than Grandfather's trees. You didn't come with us when we planted the last tree at Pete's."

For years Hank's father had planted trees everywhere in River Sunday. Since Hank had been a little boy, each year in the spring, he and his father would select a strong loblolly seedling, go out to Pete's farm, and plant it.

"No, I didn't." Hank took a chance. If the boy wanted to talk about his grandfather, he'd go along. "Tell me about it."

"Grandfather brought the tree in the back of the truck. We stopped at the general store along the road near the farm. He bought me a Coke and he got a Nehi soda like he always did. We drove over to the edge of the field behind Pete's house where the trees were."

"That first one he planted is pretty tall," said Hank.

"He said that one was set in 1947 and there's been one ever since."

"I wasn't there that day for sure."

"He said you planted your first tree in the row when you were four."

"I only remember how big the shovel was," said Hank.

"I like how the trees are slanted from the first one down to the last in a diagonal line from tall to short."

"Yes."

"We should put in a new one. We haven't planted any since he died." Bobby paused and added, "No, I don't think I want to do that."

Bobby continued, "Tell me about when he saved the firemen."

"I could tell that," said Sammy, standing next to Hank. Another fireman had taken over running the tractor. Sammy had a long measuring tape. He was trying to figure out by measuring along the side of the mound how far Bobby was away from the trench digging.

Hank handed Sammy the microphone.

"Bobby, it's the Chief," said Sammy.

"Are you working harder on the mound? I can feel the ground shaking," said Bobby.

"Tractor's getting closer to you. You tell me if the shaking gets to be too much," said Sammy. "We don't want to take any chances."

"No, it's all right. I'm just so cold," replied Bobby. "That is the worst of it down here. You guys talking to me helps a lot."

Charlie interrupted. "We've got to gas up the generator, Hank. It will only be a few minutes."

"We have to shut down for a few minutes to put in gasoline. I'll be right back, Bobby," Sammy said. Hank knew Bobby would be nervous, waiting for the radio to come back on.

He helped Charlie with the gasoline. As he was holding the container, he glanced around. Hank could see the whole operation. Behind him was the small expanse of water leading from the island to the ranger station dock and Pete's farmhouse. In between, rocking in the swells, were two or three boats picking up swimming animals. Each had lights aboard which would outline the passengers, and from time to time, someone on the boats would wash the island with a searchlight, turning the rescuers around Hank into white figures. Beyond them, in the far distance and through the reeds and mud islands, were flashing lights of twenty or more trucks and utility vehicles. Pete's porch light was still on, and every window in his house was lit.

On the island, in front of Hank, the small beach was the center of activity. Here were several outboard boats pulled up, one with a stretcher sitting on its gunwales. Behind Hank, volunteers worked hard at filling bags. They had dug out a large pit where before there had only been marsh grass and driftwood. As the bags were filled they were handed person to person along the hundred yards or so to be placed on the walls. Since he had looked before, the walls had grown another two sandbags in height all the way around.

At the far end of the mound from where he stood near the radio, the trench was larger. With the tractor and the steady work of men with shovels, the mound was definitely showing signs of being penetrated. The large ditch extended into the end of the mound thirty or so feet. As Hank had suspected, the problem continued to be shoring up the weak and wet sides of the trench as the tractor worked inward.

The generator began to run again. Sammy picked up the microphone and started to talk to Bobby. "Your grandfather's career with the River Sunday Volunteer Fire Department was a good one. He was one of the few who could handle the climb up the big extension ladder to work the high pressure hose. He had his fear of being closed in, a lot more than most of us, but no fear of height.

"No doubt, Bobby, about where you get your courage. We were never so proud of your grandfather as the night that there was the warehouse fire. These warehouses had been empty for years, left over from when River Sunday had canneries. It was a large wooden building right on the harbor."

Hank took the mike and added, "My parents and I lived in rooms behind the garden shop and nursery. I woke up and heard Daddy moving around in the next room; my mother telling him to be careful. Then I heard the delivery van start up and my father drove out the driveway towards the fire house, a mile away over back streets of small yards and residences.

"I got up and tiptoed to my window to see out at the town. I saw a glow in the sky. My heart pounded as I quickly put on my clothes. I did not stop to tell my mother for I knew she would forbid me to go. Instead I left a note on the kitchen table. Outside it was summer and the air was moist with dew and humidity, some of it from the wet air drifting in off the harbor. I could smell smoke.

"Then I was running along the side of the macadam road, my tennis shoes crashing against the high grass and the stones and gravel that was there, and the rough cracks in the soil made by rainwater runoff, hardened into sharp crevasses for me to trip against, but I kept running harder, excited and afraid, knowing Daddy would be involved in this fire."

Sammy took the mike back, "Hoses were laid all over the street and trucks were parked everywhere. The big hook and ladder truck, the most powerful in the department, was anchored against the side of the burning building. The town police held back the spectators.

"The word went out that some of our men were trapped inside the building. A huge burst of flame was shooting up through the roof. The top of the hook and ladder was right in the flame but that was where we needed the water hose. Then your grandfather came up to the ladder in his fireman's coat. He didn't hesitate but went right up that ladder where none of the other men would go. At the top of the ladder the hose nozzle glinted in the night sky, against the gray of the smoke and about fifty feet above the building with the roaring inferno coming out of the roof, licking at the rungs.

"He reached the top of the ladder. He resolutely turned the nozzle into the fire and signaled below for the other men to adjust the water flow. Then the hose spoke with a stream of water into the hissing fire. The water tore at the flames and pieces of roof timbers flew up into the air as the roof began to collapse. In time the fire began to die down and our men could get to the others trapped inside. No lives were lost. Some of the men here tonight working to get you safe have never forgotten what you grandfather did for them and their families."

Then Sammy suddenly handed Hank the mike. He spit and began running toward the tractor.

"What in the hell?" shouted the fireman driving the tractor as he frantically worked the blade lever. The engine chugged down to a last lurch and stalled.

"Choked her out, damn it," he said, getting down from the controls and moving to the front.

"You hit something," yelled Sammy who jumped down into the trench, the Captain right behind him, both of them brushing by the firemen to the front wall. Will followed as fast as he could.

Sammy said "I don't see anything." He climbed up on the tractor, started the engine and backed out from the mud wall where the blade had caught.

"I'm going to try her again, a little slower. Captain, stand by with some shovels just in case," Sammy called out. He applied the power and moved the blade up to the bank. The front of the tractor began to dance, the wheels compressing against the plywood and sandbag runway. The engine climbed in revolutions but refused to lift the blade against whatever it had contacted.

The Captain waved Sammy to slow down. He released the throttle and the tractor idled.

"Might just be a root. How long is that plane anyway, Captain?" asked Sammy.

"Sixty feet. He's about fifty feet from the sides of the mound at the other end. If the boy is where we think, the tail section could be here, close to end of the trench."

"OK to bring the tractor up again, Captain?" asked Sammy.

The Captain nodded.

The pressure on the tractor blade made the engine work very hard, almost enough to make it balk. Sammy expertly applied power, revving the engine up and down, working the controls to try to get the bucket to lift the obstruction.

Charlie turned the radio on. Bobby was calling, his voice loud. "Daddy, it's shaking here. The light just went out too. It's dark again."

Hank immediately ran toward the tractor. He waved vigorously and shouted, "Hey, Sammy, hold up down there."

Sammy was so intense on driving the tractor he did not hear Hank. By then however, the Captain, who did hear, had jumped up on the running board and switched off the ignition. The tractor trembled to a stop, steam coming off its hot engine cover as the wild rain spat against the metal.

"What in the hell?" said Sammy.

"Hank wants you to stop everything," the Captain said, his voice louder as the engine became silent. "Some of the mound is falling in on the kid."

"Good Lord," said Sammy.

Hank returned to the microphone and talked to his son. They listened as the little voice came over the speaker, the only other noise the wind and large raindrops slapping the sandbags.

Bobby's voice called out, "I'm falling!"

Then silence.

Hank called, "Bobby! Talk to me!"

It took a few tense moments but the boy finally answered, "I'm all right. The seat I was on fell down into the water. A lot of bones are around me. I can feel the skull. I also touched a pair of goggles."

"Are you hurt?"

"No, but more mud is filling in behind where I sit. I can feel it oozing. I can barely hear you. Maybe you can talk louder."

Charlie shook his head. "We got full volume power going down there, Hank."

"We'll try to speak louder, Bobby."

"The animals are swimming around."

Hank felt a hand on his shoulder. It was Betty Allingham. "Tell him to remain as still as he can."

"Betty says the animals will not bother you if you don't move."

She added, "Tell him to move slowly if he has to move at all."

"Betty says to move slowly, so the animals won't get too scared."

Bobby's voice was trembling. "Yes, they are just as scared as I am. I forgot about that."

Then he continued, "Tell Cathy I'm going to bring these goggles out for her to wear when she flies." He paused and said, "Oh golly, I think I've let out Cathy's secret. What I said went out for everybody to hear. Oh, God, she'll never forgive me."

Hank called back, "No, honey, her father wasn't listening."

"She's my friend. Don't you think she would like that, Daddy?"

"I'm sure she would like it." Hank winked at Cathy who was listening with a grin. "Try to climb out of that water."

"OK."

"Can you get hold of anything?"

"I can hold on to the seat support."

"Be careful, Bobby," Hank said.

Betty pressed the back of Hank's neck. He reached up and touched her hand.

"Thank you," he whispered. Then he called Bobby again.

"How are you doing?"

"I just wish I could see something. I keep moving my hand in the air. This was a big airplane all right. Does Captain Steele think we found the lost P47?"

"No one knows, Bobby." He heard the sound of the boy's exertions as he tried to move around in the cockpit.

Hank turned to Charlie. "What about sending down another light?"

"If we pull the other out and send down a new one, it might cause more collapse, like a small landslide next to Bobby. I don't think we ought to do it," said Captain Steele.

Then, from Bobby, "I found a place closer to the right side of the airplane to sit. I'm back out of the water again. The animals are down below me."

Hank wanted to keep hearing Bobby's voice. "Are you all right?" He didn't want to say that they could not replace the light.

Bobby said, "Thank the Chief for telling me that story." Hank knew his father was not respected when Hank was young. He was an immigrant. In a small town like River Sunday, that put him on the lowest level of society. Hank had heard his father called a displaced person, a "DP." When he was older, he found out displaced persons were like the long ago Acadians and the French trapper, people moved from their homes because of war.

Hank was a small child when he first heard the name "DP." His mother was driving him from a swimming lesson at a friend's beach outside of town. He remembered the heat that morning and that the metal dashboard of the car was hot from the sun - too hot to touch.

He could only see a little bit over the dashboard of the car. He had to sit forward on the front seat and pull himself up. A few hundred feet ahead a large harvesting machine had turned onto the narrow road from a cornfield. It was a giant red machine with a small control cab high up off the road. In that cab he could see a man smiling at them. The harvester was driving directly down the center of the road. His mother grasped the steering wheel with both hands. She had stopped singing and was muttering. He couldn't understand what she was saying. She slowed the car and blasted the horn.

"Goddamn smiles of these people. Why can't they be like your father and show some brains for a change?"

He could hear her words but did not understand them. The man was smiling at them.

The harvester began to pull to the side of the road to let his mother get by. She slowed the car more and then carefully squeezed by the huge machine, narrowly avoiding the side of her car being scraped.

He heard her say "DP" and "Jew" like it was a swear word. Then she caught herself and quickly turned to Hank. "Don't you say anything to your father. Forget that you heard me say anything about Jews and DPs."

When his father came to River Sunday after the War, he took a gardening job for the only person in River Sunday who would hire him, Missus Steers. His mother had been one of her housekeepers. Missus Steers was not popular and was considered suspicious, mostly because she was European of German heritage. Stories were made up about her, especially about Nazi submarines visiting her place at night.

The gardens at the Steers house were so big that he and Mudman thought they could ride their bikes around paths among the overgrown boxwoods and not be seen by anyone in the house. They climbed in the trees. One day Hank saw a face at one of the second story windows. It was Missus Steers, white hair all streaked out. Next to him in another tree, Mudman called, "The old lady is watching us."

"Hank," Pete's strong voice came at him and brought him back to the present. "They've got to get going on the trench."

"Bobby, we're going to dig again," said Hank into the mike.

"All right, Daddy."

Captain Steele climbed down into the shaft and walked up to the firemen who were poking at the mud with their shovels. "We'll keep on going but with smaller bites."

"Here, stand back, Captain," said Sammy, starting up the engine again. The tractor came forward again and its blade went in a few inches at a two foot distance to the left. The bucket came back out, half full of mud. One of the firemen pointed to the wall where the right side of the blade had cut.

"Hey, Captain, see what she hit into."

Captain Steele stepped up to the wall and chipped at the mud with the tip of his shovel. "Bring the light closer, boys."

Chapter Fifteen

The Captain moved his hand tenderly over the vertical edge of gray corroded metal stretching three or four feet up from the base of the mound. "It's her all right," he said, almost whispering. He grinned, like an old man who suddenly sees a long lost schoolmate at his high school reunion.

"What do we do now?" asked Sammy.

"Yank the plane out," said Will, rushing to the Captain's side. "You've got to use the tractor."

"Will, we'd kill the boy. The tractor's too hard to control," said the Captain. "We'll have to dig by hand, and carefully."

Tawny followed Duke into the trench. Bits of the walls were slipping back into the cut area and causing the men to shovel more quickly.

"How long before you reach the child?" she asked the Captain. Her cameraman began running his video.

The old aviator shook his head and continued cleaning the thin ridge of metal. "We're on the plane's left side. We could dig a tunnel right up to where the boy is located, maybe forty some feet to the cockpit," said Sammy.

"Maybe we could climb through the fuselage itself," suggested Pete.

"We could dig along and look for a way in, we could do that," said the Captain.

"Why not go in through the fuselage?" asked Will, already working with the others to dig around this metal strip.

"We are not as small as he is. I think he got into that cockpit through the ripped section when the left wing broke off. Inside we'd have to cut through all the machinery of the aircraft. The machinery is, however, what is holding the fuselage together. If the hull wasn't full of equipment, if it was hollow, in other words, it would have collapsed. Same would happen if we cut through it."

"Have you thought about unexploded bombs?" asked Sammy.

"We'll just have to be careful," said the Captain. "If there's ordnance still on her, we could get hurt, that's for sure. When we get to the plane, we'll have to check that out as best we can."

"If it's my aunt's plane, she had no ammunition, no bombs on board. That would mean no danger to us. Let's go for it," said Will.

The Captain turned and faced Sammy. "The biggest problem is digging along the left side of the hull. We might loose the fuselage from its grip on the earth, make it slide on further. The boy told us that the plane shook when it got hit by the tractor."

Pete said, "We can't stop it from moving."

"The boy will be long gone before we can get to him," nodded the Captain. "Remember, you're dealing with five tons of metal here. That big Pratt and Whitney engine on the front of her is like a lead sinker on a fishing line."

"We'd never reach him," said Hank.

The Captain checked his watch. "You wouldn't get to him before that high tide, that's for sure."

"Like I said, what do you think we ought to do, Captain?" asked Sammy.

"We could put a line around her tail and pull her out," blurted Will. "I got a winch on the tractor."

"That tail fin would break off. The metal's too corroded," said Bob Johnny.

The Captain turned around. "Will's idea might not be so far off."

"You really think that plane could be pulled out, Captain?" asked Pete.

"Not pulled out. Held was what I was thinking. It might be the only chance we have. The more we dig the more chance there is that the plane will loosen and slide into the earth. On the other hand, we can't get at him without digging."

He thought for a moment. "What I'd do is get a line around her to hold her steady. With that done, we'd have a chance to cut that tunnel beside the plane to get at the boy. No, Will, I don't think I'd try to pull her out. Too many things could go wrong."

"We're going to lose the plane if we don't do something," said Will.

"Just for once, Will, take my word for it," said the Captain.

"Then that's what we'll do, like the Captain says," Sammy ordered.

"The aircraft crashed in there. Just pull her out the same way she went in," said Will.

"Can't be too impatient, Will. We'll get Bobby out," said the Captain.

Melissa laughed. "You don't get it, Captain Steele. He doesn't care any more about Bobby than if it was me or you caught in there. He wants that plane, that's all."

Will shook his head and went back to stand by the tractor, staring at the mound. Beside him, two of Sammy's firemen were preparing the winch.

Tawny had her assistant photograph the men working on the tail section. She also spoke into her tape recorder, preparing a report for her editor. "We have a discovery here at the rescue site where the Green child has been trapped since yesterday afternoon. Rescue workers have uncovered part of what appears to be a military aircraft. This may be part of what has been the support for the child underneath the tons of mud over him. Strangely, it's the framework of an airplane lost here during World War Two."

She reached down with her recorder to interview Captain Steele who was watching as the men uncovered more of the metal slab. "Captain, is there any more identification of the airplane itself?"

"Yes, here's the trim tab," he said, pointing out a small rectangle inserted into the rudder surface. "It's definitely part of the tail of a P47 fighter."

"The child is in the forward part of this aircraft?"

"Yes Ma'am, that's what we think," said the Captain. "Some feet ahead in the cockpit."

"How will you get to the child?"

"We're going to attach lines to the aircraft tail and secure it so it will not slide forward. Then we're going to dig along the port side until we get to the boy's location. After ascertaining that, we will enter the fuselage in the best way we can without causing it to collapse or slide further."

"How did the child get there?"

"We can't say for sure. We think he followed a cave and came in through a hole on the left of the plane, looking forward. We'll dig along that side and hope we can go in the same way he did."

"Will you ever be able to tell where this P47 came from?"

"When we get some more of this tailfin cleaned off we may see some identification numbers. Most of the P47 fighters had six numbers painted on their tail. When we have the number we can trace it through military records."

She continued, "The child mentioned that he noticed bones near where he was trapped. Do you think these were the remains of Melusina

Allingham, the pilot who fought a German submarine in the Atlantic near here?"

"We don't know. Could be the pilot bailed out and those are animal bones. We just can't tell. Now, if you'll excuse me, I've got to get to work."

"Thank you. I've been speaking with Captain Steele. He is the director of the local River Sunday airport and his staff has always been most helpful to us when we fly to the Eastern Shore. We'll get back to him a little later. This is Tawny Slight reporting from River Sunday at the site of the cave-in, where the rescue team races against the incoming tide of a great coastal storm to free a young boy. Only hours remain before the storm surge and flood tide reaches the Wilderness Swamp. Then if he is not rescued, he will be drowned."

Captain Steele examined the larger piece of tail surface that had been unearthed.

"Captain Steele, this metal, it's corroded," said Sammy. "The tractor blade ain't done it no good neither."

Pete moved down into the trench and joined Hank and Sammy who were helping the Captain dig out the rudder.

"You said Bobby might have climbed in through where the wing met the fuselage?" asked Pete.

The Captain nodded in the rain. "Where it broke off. Animals coming and going probably enlarged the break."

"Where is the wing?"

"Probably in the muck beside the plane," said the Captain. "It may be lifted up and bent around."

"You're saying the tail numbers will tell us if it's my great aunt's airplane?" asked Will, coming down beside them.

"Shut up, Will," said Melissa.

"I think so, Will," answered the Captain.

"Her number was 222222," Will said. "One of the earlier models, the razorbacks."

"What is a razorback?" asked Tawny, pulling out her notebook.

"On the early models, the cockpit extended directly back to the tail fin. Later designs had a bubble canopy to allow the pilot better vision in all directions."

Most of the tail section including the rudder and part of the left elevator had been uncovered and stuck out in the rain. The dug out shaft or tunnel below the tail structure had increased in size.

Will had found a ladder and was scraping at the metal of the rudder. "Captain, I can see a number here," Will said.

"Get him some more light," said the Captain, standing up to inspect the metal.

Among the streaks was the number 2 in white surrounded by a bluish paint.

"That's part of the identification number anyway," said the Captain. "The rest of it is obscured in the corrosion."

"Metal experts can bring out those other numbers," said Will. He kicked at the muck with his boot. "If only Bobby could've told us more about that skeleton."

Hank could see Melissa staring at Will, showing her amazement at Will's excitement about his plane while her child was in such peril.

Captain Steele motioned to Sammy. "We'll have to dig more on that shaft under the plane. We've got to find a strong point where we can latch our lines."

Sammy shook his head.

Steele tried to reassure him. "I think the airplane will stay together, Sammy. They were built real strong."

Pete pointed to the power take off winch on the tractor. "Is Will right about there being enough power to hold back the weight of the plane?"

"Enough to bring it snug," said Sammy.

"Might want to rig some teams on ropes pulling too," suggested Pete.

The Captain nodded. "That's a good idea. Sammy, let's have your strongest men on some ropes."

"It's going to be dangerous for Bobby," said Hank.

"You've got to save my son," demanded Melissa.

Hank glanced at Melissa. "This is all we can do."

She stared back at him. "Then we have to do it."

Hank nodded.

Hank joined the others digging under the rudder and the stern fuselage to find a grip point for the lines.

"Can you see anything more?" asked Will.

The Captain pointed to several small holes in the metal. "She ran into flak here. Zinnie's plane circled the submarine for a long time and she took some fire." He proceeded to dig at the metal with his penknife, talking to Will as he did so.

"You surprise me, Will. Always have. You went and built that model of your aunt's plane for the parade. From what I hear you're an authority on P47s. You're an expert about war but you never faced an enemy bullet."

"I was in the Guard," Will said, his eyes searching the old metal.

"Zemke's Wolfpack." That's what the B17 bomber crews called us when we escorted them over Germany," said the Captain. "Me, Gabreski, Robert Johnson, Schilling, Christensen, Mahurin. All the aces."

The Captain traced his fingers over the rudder. "You have any idea why I won't get inside that airplane float you build every year for the Heritage Day? It's because I know that you don't do it to honor any of us or even Zinnie, Will. You do that to get people to look for her plane so you can get some land."

Will seemed not to hear the Captain. He looked impatient that the work was not going faster. Hank thought Will no longer had any pride left - that the man had become willing to grovel to all of them, not for the child, but to get the P47 out of the mound.

The Captain extracted a slug that he had been digging from the rudder material. "Here, Will." He held it up for Will to see. "That's a 37 millimeter round. The Germans used that caliber on their submarines. I know because I got hit with these rounds flying too low over an enemy sub in the Channel."

As Hank knew he would, Will immediately asked as soon as the Captain stopped talking, "Are you going to help me salvage this plane, Captain?"

With that, the Captain threw the spent bullet on the ground in disgust. Then he said, brushing off his hands, "Will, I'm here to help Hank's boy. I'm not saying I don't love these old fighter planes. I flew one like her. Helping you, though, is, for me, like being a traitor to Zinnie's memory. If salvaging her means making you rich, I'd rather let the plane stay where it is."

"What happens if the airplane slips down, way down, too deep to retrieve?"

"If we get the boy out, and the plane is lost forever, that's all right with me," said the Captain.

"If there's danger the boy will be lost, you ought to give him a chance to make his confession," said a voice behind Hank.

"Father Tom." It was the priest from the church Hank attended.

"Yes, Father. I want you to talk to him," said Melissa.

The priest put his hand on Melissa's arm. "It will be all right."

Bobby began to scream again. The sound came out of the big speakers and wailed all over the island. "The muskrats are all over me. Please get me out of here."

Hank called him on the microphone. "I'm here."

"I'm so scared, Daddy. You're coming down here to get me out?"

"I sure am."

"What about your claustrophobia?"

"Fathers can handle things like that."

"Please come get me."

"I will."

"Father Tom wants to talk to you, Bobby."

"All right."

Hank remembered Father Tom's words at the garden store one afternoon. Just back from mission work down in Peru, the priest had come into Hank's store and said, "Hank, I'd like to put a flower or two in a little space, a little devotional garden, behind the church. I want annuals," the priest had insisted.

"Why?"

"I want something new each year." He went on and said, "I remember a garden like this when I was in a little country south of here. It was next to a new graveyard. I used to sit in that garden and study the graveyard. You see," he had said to Hank, "I witness death all the time. I hear the last confessions and I give the last rites. I need more birth, much more."

Hank had said, "You need more hope."

Father Tom replied, "Yes, hope."

In the rain, as if reading Hank's mind, the priest said, "We'll talk, Bobby and I, of hope."

The priest crowded into the radio tent with Melissa and Hank. He took the mike, "Hi Bobby."

"You'll talk about Easter tomorrow," began Bobby.

"Jesus on the cross."

"Did Jesus have a grandfather?"

"In a way he did."

"Tell me about hate, Father."

"Hate means you want to kill someone."

"Is there any other kind of hate?"

"Not really, Bobby," said Father Tom.

"I guess I don't hate anyone."

"We should be like Jesus," offered Father Tom.

"What would Jesus do if someone lied to him?" asked Bobby.

"He'd forgive him. That's what love is all about," answered the priest.

"That's hard to do."

"Yes," answered Father Tom. "Very hard to be like Jesus. Can you confess with me?"

"I'm not going to die. I got no reason," answered Bobby. Then he asked, "Father, is this place I'm in like hell?"

"It might be, Bobby. It might be."

"I've got something to do, Father."

"Can I help you?"

"No, I've got to do it myself and pretty soon."

"Then ask Jesus to help you."

"I will, Father Tom."

The priest took out his crucifix of silver and prayed silently.

The Captain called Hank. "We're just about ready back here. I want to talk to Bobby before we start." Lightning sparked close to the island. Hank mentally counted, one thousand, two thousand. Then the thunder tore into the swamp, echoing against the loblollies and rumbling its terror, its wild noise. He thought about Bobby under the ground. He can't hear that noise. No, maybe he can and he doesn't recognize it. Then he thought, of course he knows what it is.

The rain, suddenly harder, was slapping Hank's face. "Come on, Hank," Pete was calling. "We need you on the ropes."

"I'll be right there," Hank said and went faster along the slippery path beside the sandbags. He noticed the water was higher, almost to his knees.

"Water," he said to one of the sandbag team members as he went by.

"So far so good," the woman replied, her face small in her poncho. The lightning smashed the sky again and lit the island brighter than the biggest searchlights the firemen had installed. The raindrops were large and spattered against Hank, slowing him as he moved toward the winch.

Chapter Sixteen

Hank listened as the Captain laid out the plan. The tractor idled in the background, rhythmic against the storm roar. They were squatting in a circle in front of the tractor. Captain Steele was explaining the construction of the plane and how best to attach the winch to the fuselage. Hank helped Sammy hold a piece of canvas to shield the rain from the well-creased paper drawings of the aircraft spread out on the plywood tractor runway. Pete held the large flashlight.

The Captain began. "Assuming that now we know for sure where the plane is and how it lies in the mud, we have a chance that we didn't have before. We're not going in blind any more." He opened a large manual. "The rudder extended up over the fuselage about six feet, as tall as a man. I can picture my wartime mechanic standing on a ladder near the elevators and adjusting a clevis bolt on the rudder link." He paused and looked at the diagram before proceeding.

"We want to attach as far into the fuselage as we can. I'd be happier if we could get beyond the tail assembly and into the forward fuselage maybe to this lifting tube." He pointed to the cross brace built into the frames, a little bit ahead of the tail. "That's a strong point to get near if we can."

Hank looked at Sammy. "Let's get started finding that point. We'll dig further under her," he said, moving to join the men working under the fuselage.

After a few minutes, Hank clambered out and said, "We got a break in the metal about two feet further in. We can get a hook attached."

"Let me see," said the Captain. "I need some light back in there."

Pete handed him the flashlight. Captain Steele crawled down beside Hank and reached back into the muck, feeling with his hand, then pulling back.

"Your spot is good, Hank. It's in the hull near where the lifting area should be and that's a plus." He stood up.

"OK," said Hank, ready to go back under the airplane. "Get me a line in here." The men passed him the wire from the winch. A large hook was at the end of the cable.

The Captain kneeled by Hank, holding in front of him a page from his manual showing that part of the fuselage, explaining that the hook and wire had to go around the nearest fuselage frame member. Hank nodded as he crawled under again. He pulled the wire after him into the hole. The cable made a scraping sound as the wire rubbed against the metal of the airplane.

"Gimme more."

"Run out the winch," ordered Sammy. There was a squeal as the pulley spun.

In a few minutes Hank crawled out. "OK, that's got it," said Hank, pulling the wire taut behind him. He stood up and said to the Captain, "I got it inside the fuselage and looped around the brace in the tail. I can feel where the tail wheel assembly fell out."

"The casting that Cathy found," nodded the Captain.

Hank stood next to Pete. "One thing I noticed, though. The rudder assembly may be bent backward. That fuselage below it is set at an angle to the rudder. In other words, the rudder is aimed down but the fuselage is angled up. I think she broke her rudder when she hit, then tipped down by her nose."

That worried the Captain. "If we get her at the wrong angle, we might tilt her more downward," he said. "Worse, we might crack the fuselage in another place with the wrong pressure on the hull frames."

"We'll build up a leverage point to pull the rope over," said Sammy. "That should keep her held back at the right angle when we dig."

"Yeah, that's a good idea," said Hank. "Then after we start the tunnel to Bobby we can reconnect, move the wire loop further down the fuselage, and make it even more secure."

Sammy had the tree men clean up three logs from the cut loblollies. "We'll need them about the width of the trench."

The rain made it hard to see. When the trees were brought over to the tractor area, Pete and Sammy had the men lay them below the rudder section. The men roped them together and slung down from the center a block and tackle.

The angle was crucial, the Captain insisted. He had Hank and the others measure as carefully as possible the perspective of the fuselage direction. Then a line from the aircraft was put down through the block and back and up to the winch which was about four feet above it. As he explained it, the cable would come out from the aircraft and be directed towards the ground of the trench. The pressure on the aircraft would be in the same direction in which she lay.

The Captain was satisfied but Sammy wanted safety lines. "We can get men to pull along with the tractor. The lines may be needed to guide the fuselage if she starts to move from side to side."

Sammy had several of his firemen line up with ropes attached to the airplane. One of the chainsaw men, a large man with a beard, took the lead on one of the ropes. Hank headed up the other, on the right side. Will, who had been standing to the side with Melissa, watching all this planning going on without saying anything, came forward.

"Sammy, you should let me run that winch."

"I thought you didn't want to drive the tractor, Will."

"I've pulled out a lot of stumps and muskrat houses with that winch. Maybe you ought to let me handle it so it doesn't burn out."

Sammy glanced towards Hank and the others. "You sure, Will?"

Will's face drew up tight in anger. "You guys steal my tractor. Now you tell me I can't even get on it?"

"Let him handle the winch, Sammy," said Pete. "We need someone who knows the machine on this kind of job."

"You'll see," said Will.

"Well, come on, get over with me," said Sammy. The winch control was beside Sammy, a lever on the metal floor of the tractor.

"The winch has enough power for what we want," said the Captain. "Just pull the line taut and hold it there, Will. We don't want the fuselage pulled out, just held tight so we can work on getting down beside it. Then, as the men dig, we may have to adjust the tension. Sammy, you might want to keep the tractor in gear in case the power of the transmission is also needed to pull back on the wheels in reverse. Everything has to be slow. Even tightening up on her might start her moving. We need to be careful. You got that, Will?"

Will nodded.

Captain Steele stood near the tail section and inspected the ropes and the winch cable. Hank was beside him.

"Hank, I realize you're worried. You got to have faith. We always have risk in any rescue, no matter what."

Hank nodded. "Just talk to Bobby," he said. "He's going to be so scared in there."

Bobby listened while the Captain explained on the radio what they were going to do. "When we put a tight line on the fuselage to hold it steady, you may feel something."

"That's all right, Captain Steele."

Hank added, as the Captain switched off the mike, "If the airframe holds together."

Pete said, putting his hand on Hank's shoulder, "Maybe later we will find out that there was a better way. I say let's try it anyway and maybe the Lord will be with us."

Hank turned to Melissa. She said, "You decide, Hank. You tell me what to do."

Tawny's cameraman turned on his video. Tawny and Duke stood by the wall of sandbags watching, she with her microphone in hand, her mouth open ready to speak.

"You give the signal, Hank," said Sammy. "It's your call."

"All right. Everyone ready?" asked Hank. Then he motioned to Will to start the winch. The assembled group watched as the line worked through the block and tackle and began to take up slack against the fuselage. Hank as well as the other linemen pulled hard on their steering cables. The line was almost taut.

Sammy said, "Ease her, Will."

Before Sammy could say any more, before the line put any pressure on the hulk, the plane started to slip forward into the muck, first a half inch or so then an inch and more. Hank's worst fear had occurred. The old fuselage, the broken rudder, all were trembling the mound surface, ripples heading in all directions in the soft wet surface.

"Good Jesus," said Sammy. "She's moving down on her own. We got the ropes on just in time. Hold taut on the winch and the hand lines."

Over the wind noise and the pelting rain, the old fuselage metal creaked.

Will applied the winch. The sliding process reversed. The rudder was coming to the surface, further out than before, much further. A whole section that had been covered before was seen, the area of the number and the section beside it with the corrosion and even more. More bullet holes could be seen in the lower part of the rudder assembly.

The Captain called out, "Will, you're pulling the damn thing out. Don't wind that winch any more. We just want it back where it was. You're pulling too hard."

Hank saw Will bent over the control lever, his eyes on the moving rudder as it came out of the mud into the air.

Hank screamed, "Stop it, Will, damn you. Somebody stop him!" He let go his line to the man behind him and started toward Will.

Will kept his hands tightly on the control lever. Sammy was reaching down, trying to free the lever from Will's grasp.

A section of fuselage was easing out of the mound with bits of earth and streams of water running down its sides. Slowly, an inch more was exposed, then another inch, then an area of bent and corroded metal with some large holes in a staggered pattern. Part of a striped United States insignia with the edge of a white star came into view.

"You damn fool. You're winching too hard on purpose!" Hank had almost reached Will.

The noise suddenly increased to a shriek, and the winch drum began smoking. Captain Steele hollered "Shut it down, Shut it down. You're going to lose the plane!"

It was too late.

With a wrenching noise the clutch of the winch burned out and the drum ran free. At the mound, the rudder and the rest of the fuselage immediately started to sink back. The end of the line whipped through the block and into the mound surface, hitting boards and sandbags with loud noises and clanks, spattering muck. The other lines that had held the fuselage pulled taut but the men were not able to hold them. The ropes wrenched from their hands and slipped back into the mud wall like snakes going into their holes until only small portions of the twisted and broken ends were sticking out. The remains of the fuselage had disappeared with the water and mire seething back over it like a closing door.

Finally it stopped moving.

Hank pulled Will down from the tractor and shoved him against a tire, shaking him against the cleats and hitting his face over and over. Blood spurted out of Will's mouth and nose as he tried to fend off Hank.

"You killed him, you bastard. You just killed Bobby," Hank screamed as he hit Will again. "On top of that you might have set off some damn bombs on her and blown all of us to hell, you damn fool."

The Captain and Pete pulled Hank away. Will slumped against the tire then slid down to the ground, water along his legs and almost to his waist. He moved his hands slowly over his face, rubbing away the blood.

"I wanted to hit him, too, Hank," said Sammy. "Then I realized that there's no sense to it. He ain't worth anything and never will be."

Pete said, "I don't know what more we can do, my friend." He called to Charlie at the radio tent. "Try to get to Bobby"

"I'm calling, "Charlie yelled over the wind.

Hank looked over with haunted eyes. "You think it's hopeless, too, Pete?"

"We don't know how far that airplane is going to slide. Of course, we can guess bombs aren't on her because nothing went off with all that shaking. Unfortunately, not much holding her from starting again and going right on down into a real deep part. Then we can't hope to get the boy out."

"Forty, fifty, a hundred feet down. P47 airplanes were heavy. She would sink by the nose, I'm sure, right Captain?" asked Hank, rubbing his fist that had hit Will.

"I'm afraid so. I think what happened is those broken wings caught the earth when we were pulling. I was worried about that. They opened outward and held just like anchor spokes against the mound."

"We might try to dig after her," said Hank.

"If we did that it would probably sink just as we got near to it," said the Captain.

"That old wreck must have been just sitting there on the edge, ready to slip lower and we helped it go," said Sammy.

"We had no way of knowing," said Pete. "We took a chance, that's all."

"Well, I'm still for trying to dig something. We can get the dig teams set back up and start in by hand to see what we can find, that is, until she starts slipping again. We'll have to dig by hand. Can't risk using the tractor any more," said Sammy.

"Follow those ropes," said Hank.

"Yeah. We know how long the ropes were. Judging from them, I expect that she is in thirty feet more."

"Tipped a little bit more to the bottom," said Hank.

"I think it's probably both," said the Captain. "From the lengths of rope that went in, I guess she has moved ahead maybe ten feet and then she might have gone in to the ground about ten feet."

"So she's down deeper and Bobby is facing straight down into the ground," said Hank.

"The plane is in a dive attitude, yes, I think so," said Captain Steele.

"Maybe we can find something of the tunnel still and at least crawl in to where he is," said Sammy.

"Not much chance of doing that is there, Pete?" asked Melissa.

"You want the truth?" he said.

She nodded.

"No, I'm afraid there isn't much chance left, Melissa. We got the same problem we had before we tried to hold her back, only it's worse now. I'm sorry."

The television reporter began. "This is Tawny Slight reporting from River Sunday where the last chapter of a great tragedy has just begun. For the last hour the combined rescue teams and Federal Park Rangers have tried to pull an old warplane out of the earth. The airframe, caught in the swamp for more than fifty years, is holding a small boy who crawled into it through a cave here last evening. While the best minds available had rigged the extraction process no one could have foreseen that all hope would be lost when the winch and ropes broke loose and the plane plunged down, carrying the child too deep for the rescue to continue. The wreck has stopped moving so we are waiting to see if it starts again into the depths of the Wilderness."

"Chief, what will you and the others do?" asked Tawny.

Sammy answered, spitting, "We will pray that we get to the boy before our time runs out."

"We will pray too, Captain Steele. Thank you," said Tawny and then she motioned to her photographer, "Cut."

Tears were coming down Melissa's cheeks. "How long will your men continue to do that work on the sandbags? I mean how much longer will you be trying to get my boy?"

"Well, I don't rightly know," said Sammy. "Water's coming in more. We might be able to keep on going for a while. Then, we will have to make a guess as to what chance the boy still might have."

"I'll pay to keep men digging," Melissa said, sobbing.

"Well it's not so much a case of that. It is whether we got a reason to keep on going. You remember when we started we did not know whether he was alive. Then we heard him talk and that kind of proved that we was right to dig here in the first place. We need something else to happen to give us some encouragement that we can succeed."

"If it doesn't happen?" she asked.

"We'll have to make a decision that all of us agree on."

"You'll talk to us before you stop trying to find him?" asked Hank.

"We'll talk. One thing that's going to hurt us, though."

"What's that, Sammy?" asked Hank.

"We don't know whether we are going to be able to hold back this flood water."

"What about the sandbags?" she asked.

"They might hold for a while. If it comes on to blow real hard and the surge comes in with the tide, we can't win."

"Is there anything more that we can do?" asked Hank.

"We are doing all we can."

"If the water breaks through to the mound?" Melissa asked, staring at the ground.

"Let's us worry about that when we get there," said Sammy.

"How much longer before the tide is full?" asked Melissa.

"Well," Sammy scanned the marsh, "the Coast Guard has been on the radio saying that the big water will be here soon." He walked toward the sandbag wall. "You men know the risk. I want only volunteers here. The rest of you can head back to your families."

As he spoke several firemen picked up their shovels and began to dig again in the collapsed trench.

Sammy said, "Melissa, you come over here. Hank, you ought to see this too." She walked slowly toward the wall, hesitant.

Hank did not move. He already knew.

Sammy pointed outside the wall where the water had risen to half the height of the stacked sandbags, The sandbags had only about two feet margin over the top of the marsh water level.

"The water is getting higher. It gets rough in spurts," said Sammy.

"What do you mean?" asked Melissa.

"You get some wind behind it in big gusts and that water will hit like a bulldozer. Those sandbags will go sliding in every direction. That's what my worry is." He continued, "I got to be sure that my men are safe." He moved his arm around. "We got our rescue workers out here working on this job and a lot of equipment, tools, that kind of thing. We get a sudden flooding out here if the wind picks up and some of the people may get hurt, maybe drowned."

"I understand," she said slowly.

"Don't you worry, I ain't given up yet."

"Thank you," she said.

Hank knelt, a shovel beside him, at the wall in front. He put his face in his hands. The rain was falling more bitterly." I don't know what more I can do," he said in prayer. "Lord, show me a way to save my son."

"Hope we still have time," said Pete.

Betty came up to Hank. "Bobby will be all right," she said.

"Betty, you don't understand. We don't even have a plan to go forward. I've got to think of what I can say to Bobby."

Duke and Tawny were inspecting the barge damage. Hank heard them talking.

"So we have it all," said Duke. "Here is the final war. Nature against the best that men can put up against it and nature wins this time."

Then Duke paused for a moment and said. "Wait a minute. Maybe it's the machine, the airplane, that's winning here. The machine that we designed to kill other men turns around and kills us. An ironic moment. On top of that, ask yourself. What is more the killer here today, the wrath of nature at being tampered with or the impersonal machine that has no soul. Neither is loyal to us. Either can just as easily kill us."

"I've read some of your editorials about nature's power. This time, you're implying that the airplane wreck has a life of its own?" asked Tawny.

Duke nodded. "An interesting concept."

"It's an old warplane continuing to hunt down prey. That's a little too heavy for my editor."

Duke smiled. "I've lived here a long time, Tawny. Seen a lot. Just lay my editorializing off to that."

Tawny moved toward the boats to go to shore. "It's pretty much over out here. I'm going."

Hank heard Duke follow her to the water's edge.

"I'll let you know what happens," Duke said to her. "I don't think I've ever seen anyone get rescued once they are buried in the mud. Besides that, the storm is going to be one of the worst in years. We almost never get storms this bad coming in the spring. The rescue is dangerous enough but with the storm, too, I think it's pretty near impossible."

Will, his face with a small bandage over the nose, had stayed near his tractor, its wheels inches in water. His goal seemed to be to retrieve at least part of the rudder that showed the number. If he could get that he could have it analyzed. He kept muttering to anyone who would listen he was sorry for what had happened, that it was an urge to try to get the aircraft out and that he thought the winch could do it. He was wrong and he was sorry.

Hank saw the growing puddles of water. An image of his past, of another funeral, the one for his father and mother, came into his mind. Their deaths came on the highway near a small intersection at a single lane highway. His father and mother were going at highway speed on the main road and a farmer drove directly in front of them from a side road without stopping. They had no chance to brake. Their car was destroyed and they were killed instantly. Hank remembered going to the funeral home and seeing them together. The whole fire department turned out. Sammy had stood up at the side of the casket, his right hand on the polished wood, Father Tom to his left.

Sammy started talking. "I guess I should say something. This man's been our boss at the department for a lot of years. We'll miss him. I'd like to share something a lot of you don't even know about him. Many of you folks don't remember the early days when this good man came to River Sunday.

"Back there, we'd go to the movies with our families. There was one night we were all there and the manager went to the stage and turned on the lights, a special intermission he told us. He was a short fat man as I remember.

"He said that he was announcing the beginning of a fund to build a monument in front of the River Sunday Courthouse that would be in honor of Melusina Allingham for her bravery in taking on and helping to sink a German submarine. He said that his ushers were going to come row by row and we ought to put in whatever we could to help raise the money. My father next to me reached in to his pocket and took out ten dollars. I remember the amount because that was a lot of money in those days.

Sammy had raised his hand slightly over the casket of Hank's father. "This man was there too, not married then, sitting all by himself in one of the back rows. He stood up and nobody noticed him for a while. When the manager was just about ready to come down off the stage, one of his ushers pointed to Hank's father.

"You have something to say, Mister Green?" the manager had asked.

"I give five hundred dollars," Hank's father had said and sat down.

"Well," said Sammy, "We heard a murmur in that theatre, voices breaking louder talk and lots of people glancing around at this man. It was true enough. The usher went over to him and received a personal check for five hundred dollars.

"The reason I tell you this story is that this man was so poor in those days he barely had money to eat. He took what money he had saved, however, and put it towards a project that meant a lot to his adopted town. I've never forgotten his kindness."

Hank remembered that after the funeral he had approached the old desk in his father's office with some hesitation. He had been standing by the desk so many times of the years to get his allowance or to get money for some errand his mother wanted him to run, and then later, as a partner in the store, to get his salary. It was a strange feeling to stand there with his father and mother just buried. He felt like a thief as he sat down at the desk and began to glance through his father's papers. One of the papers required for probate was a birth certificate or some official document indicating who his father was for the final records. Because his father had been a displaced person, he had documentation showing when he had been admitted to the United States and when he was given citizenship. The letters of transfer from Argentina to Canada then to Maryland were in order along with all the business records. His mother kept the accounts. She had even made a folder that showed every repair that had ever been done to the old van.

The desk was a large one and he searched dutifully through all the drawers and cubbyholes. There was one final drawer that had proved hard to open so he had left it for last. It was a small drawer to the right side of the desk. He used a small penknife to pry at the drawer and finally it popped open. Inside was a carefully folded piece of paper.

It was a handwritten note from Mrs. Steers to his father, faded brown, the ink writing gray. "Dear Mister Green," it began. "We met when you immigrated by sea from the old country. We spoke of the past glory many times. Never forget your bravery." The letter ended with the simple, "as always, Missus Steers."

Like all children, he wished he had been able to ask his father about her note and what she meant. He wondered about it.

The rain had picked up. Hank kneeled in the puddle and prayed, for he did not know what else to do. Father Tom came and stood beside him.

"You think God has forsaken Bobby," said the priest.

Hank replied, "I don't know."

"Even when he was facing death, Jesus had faith."

Hank felt the water slapping his legs and knew he had to stand up, somehow get the energy and hope so that he could dig again. Betty helped him up.

"I've got to talk to Bobby on the radio," he said, staring at her. Then he heard Sammy calling from the radio tent on the other side of the mound.

"Hank, can you hear me?" Sammy then began coughing.

"Sammy," Hank replied. The wind gusted harder and the rain tore into Hank's face as he listened.

"Hank," Sammy said, between coughs, "The radio line, it's gone dead. Charlie thinks it snapped when the plane moved. We can't reach Bobby."

Chapter Seventeen

"God Damn, Hank, it's almost Easter Sunday. Easter vacation's going to be over. Seem like we got to get that boy of yours home."

Hank glanced at Melissa as he heard Mudman's rough but warm voice, coming from behind him in the darkness and rain. The light humor in the voice was also standard Mudman, his way of offsetting his own demons and melancholy.

Melissa's face brightened as she also recognized the voice. Hank could sense that she, like him, like Betty and all the rest of them, immediately felt better, that all the childhood team was together again. This was the four of them from the old days when they shared the innocent attitude that anything was possible. He knew that if the luck of this rescue was going to improve, Mudman's strength was going to improve it.

Hank turned and as he did, Cincy called out, "I told you I'd get him here."

"I didn't think Cincy could get you awake in time," Hank said. He spoke slowly, almost not ready to believe that Mudman had arrived and still numbed from the failure to keep the aircraft from slipping further into the mud.

"When she told me it was about your boy, I woke up quick enough." Hank's friend was dressed in oil-stained blue jeans and a sweater with an orange windbreaker. He had on large hip boots with the tops rolled down. The windbreaker was pulled tightly around the oval of his face and the water from the rain trickled off the ridges of his cheekbones.

"Nobody was getting through the roads," Hank said, hope slowly spreading warmth through his body in the wind and rain.

"Pretty hard to stop my Harley," Mudman grinned. He had sobered up, Hank could tell. In 'Nam Mudman sobered quick when he faced danger, when each time he would not allow himself to let down his fellow soldiers.

Betty had gone over to join Cincy. Mudman's wife was covered from head to ankles in a green slicker, her legs coated with mire, bare feet sticking out at the bottom like rough brown roots.

Melissa nodded to Cincy and stared at the radio, still waiting for any sound from Bobby.

Mudman said, "I never seen such a crowd of worn out rescue people in my life" He put his hand on Hank's shoulder. "I passed boats with a lot of the men heading home."

"It's bad," said Hank.

"No one's got any ideas?"

Hank shook his head. Pete and Sammy walked up and Sammy explained the situation.

"So there was an old airplane stuck back up in that old burial mound," said Mudman. "I see Allingham's here figuring it's Zinnie's plane. Probably came as soon as he heard about the wreck."

"He's over at the former trench we cut. He wants to hook on to it again but it's too far down in the mud now."

Mudman smiled. "Will never did have much sense."

Sammy nodded. "He didn't have much luck, neither, finding it and then losing it again. 'Course it was his own damn fault."

Mudman stamped on the ground where he stood, a few feet inside the ring of sandbags. His boots splashed water and made large holes in the path.

"Trouble is," he said, looking down at his boots, "We got no bottom out here. You put a piece of iron out here, come back in a month and you'll never find it."

"We're still keeping back the water. We got a little time," said Hank.

"I don't think digging a new trench is going to accomplish anything," said Mudman. "What about that plane having unexploded bombs on her?"

"We're hoping that it's Zinnie's plane. If so, it was unarmed when she went down." He shrugged. "Not much else we can do," he said. "We just didn't want to quit, that's all. Some of the ropes are coming out the end of the old trench wall. They haven't moved any more - would have disappeared if she had slid too far. I figure she's stopped sinking for a while anyway. Far as the bombs, nothing has gone off yet and she's been bounced around a lot. The mud will protect us pretty much even if she did blow."

"Yeah," said Mudman, "Like you say, though, there's a risk of starting her moving again. Maybe you ought to stop Will from poking around back there."

Sammy shrugged. "He's working by himself with a shovel and the way that muck comes back in, he won't get very far or do any damage."

"All right." Mudman stepped to the side of the mound and studied the surface toward the hole where the thin black microphone wire was trailing into the mound. Cathy and Richard were still there too, huddled on their small pieces of plywood, watching the small hole.

Mudman walked toward the graveyard, stepping carefully beside the remaining volunteers who were still packing sandbags. Swamp water was dripping over the top bags and into the narrow walkway. Mudman splashed water. On the graveyard end where the island had the high ground for packing sandbags, some dry land still existed.

Sammy called to one of his men standing near at the sandbag wall. "Get him light. Move one of the spotlights over."

Hank asked, "What are you going to do?"

Mudman winked at Hank. "The muskrats get in there, don't they?"

Melissa put her hand on Hank's right shoulder. He turned slightly to acknowledge her presence.

Duke said, "Trappers been after muskrats around these holes for centuries. Unfortunately one of our own is caught down in them and we don't know any trappers who can figure out how to get him out."

Pete frowned. "Shut up, Duke."

"Doesn't make any difference. You stick around and you'll see plenty of muskrats coming out of the mound, when the water gets higher," said Duke.

Mudman's face was toward the graveyard "Listen. Duke's reading my mind. I've got an idea."

Hank looked up. "Go ahead."

"Rats can get down to where Bobby is located because they don't collapse the mound, right?"

Sammy nodded. "Yeah. We're too heavy. We'd push down on him or start the plane moving again. We already thought of that."

"I'm talking about the idea of being suspended, like you were being hanged, but from the feet or the waist."

Hank realized what Mudman was thinking "I get it," he said. "You suspend us as we go down into the mound."

Sammy's eyes lit up. "Right," he said, catching on. "If you hang a man so he can work from the end of a rope support, that way he don't put any weight on the mound, and he don't move the airplane. Besides, if any bombs are down there, you got a better chance of not setting them off."

"Yeah," said Mudman, "We hang and dig."

Hank added, "Besides, if it levels out then we dig level and if it slants down, then we dig down on a slant."

"We follow the mike wire," said Pete. "Right along the muskrat hole, wherever it leads."

"Yes, but you're not digging, old man," said Sammy. "This is for volunteers only. If the tunnel collapses, the rope might not get you out fast enough. You could suffocate. Too much risk."

"We shore it up as we go," said Mudman. "It won't be loose all the way. Pretty soon you'll get to firmer soil. We'll shore it up with two by fours precut maybe one foot high and three feet across. Put a bunch of them in a sack to take along and jam into place."

"How you figuring on getting a man out?" asked Sammy.

"Like in a harness. We can pull him back out easy," Mudman said, turning to Hank and the others, "We know the radio line is down there near Bobby. It went down that hole. We follow the line as far as we can. I figure we'll be near the boy and the part of the plane he's caught inside."

"The plane slid forward. The line's broken. Maybe it's not near the hole," said Charlie.

Hank reminded him, "It's the last best chance we got to find him."

Sammy brought his remaining men in closer. He said, "I need some of you that want to go down in the muskrat hole where we have the wire. You'll crawl in with a rope around your feet. We'll rig you with a radio to keep in touch with us."

"Like working in the narrow passages of a cave," said one of the firemen.

"Same thing, "said Mudman. "You'll have to work fast. At any sign of a cave in, we'll pull you right back out so you won't be buried for long, if at all."

"What if you can't get us out?"

"Always the chance," said Sammy.

"Are you going in, Mudman?" asked one of the firemen.

"I'll do my share."

"I'm going down too," said Melissa.

Hank, astonished, stared at her.

Mudman continued, "It's slow work, but we can burrow in like the rats and maybe get through before the wreck slides any further."

"I'm going down too, Pete," said Hank.

"You won't be any good to us, Hank," said Mudman.

"I've got to help my boy. This is his last chance."

"What happens if you get down there and freeze up?" asked Pete. "Better think about it, Hank."

"I'll do my job."

Pete stared at him then smiled, "I believe you will."

At Sammy's direction, several more sheets of thick plywood were laid over the soft top of the mound near the hole.

"These will give us some support. We'll use the kids like before, to help guide the lines," he said. "They don't weigh so much."

A fireman was sent down near the old trench location to check out the tractor for pulling on the rope. He reported that it was mostly under water and useless. He also advised Will to leave the spot for higher ground.

Will did not answer - just kept on shoveling.

"He won't quit," said Melissa.

"OK. I want volunteers," said Sammy, ignoring Will's stubbornness.

Charlie came up to Pete. "We've rigged headphones and a mike for them to carry down in the hole with them. We can keep some kind of check on how they are doing when they get way down inside the mound."

Sammy had some of his men bring up the three poles previously used to pull on the aircraft. Two of the poles were arranged end first along the sides of the mound with their tips meeting. The third pole was pointed to the end of the mound away from the trench. The tips were joined with rope. The block and tackle was checked and attached. Sammy and his remaining men managed to guide the posts into position. Meanwhile Mudman arranged the block and tackle so that it fell over the muskrat hole.

"Human power to pull the man up," said Hank.

Mudman smiled, lining up the ropes near him on the ground. "Me and whoever else is still around."

Melissa watched as Mudman finished adjusting the hoist. She did not speak, just stood there. Missus Pond approached the landing, her boat full of rescued animals.

She called out, "I see some of the firemen coming home. Is it all over?"

"Just volunteers left," said Sammy. "We're going to keep trying."

"I know about people running out on helpless animals. Maybe it's time you let me help," said Mrs. Pond.

Sammy paused. Pete nodded.

"Can you carry more sandbags out here?" asked Sammy.

"I'll get you some," said Mrs. Pond.

Betty called out, "I'll load the bags with you." She waded toward the boat.

The tall woman poled her boat closer to the shoreline and into the light. She was dressed in her full length rain suit, the wide brim hat drawn tightly around her face, her large eyeglasses dripping rainwater, her face solemn.

"I see Mudman," she said.

Betty climbed aboard and said, "He just arrived to help us."

"You're lucky you got him working. He'll do well for you, because he cares about the weak ones."

At that moment lightning struck nearby, toppling another tree into the swamp, light sparking on the water as the flaming tree crashed. The others threatened the trench area where Will still worked. The thunder hurtled against the rescuers, the rain gusting again as the noise echoed over the swells rising against the sandbags.

Duke took a photograph and said to Pete. "Really says it, doesn't it? I mean, tells who is going to win out here."

"Nothing is that simple, Duke," said Pete.

"Sure it is," said Duke. "I'd take the animals over the kid, and nature will beat anything these guys can do."

The two of them watched for a moment as Missus Pond slowed her boat engine on her way back to shore. She then circled around and, before proceeding again, she and Betty bent over the side to help another swimming muskrat.

Chapter Eighteen

"I respect what you're trying to do, Mudman," said Sammy, "I's worried about the safety of my people. Suppose they get down there digging on their bellies and that big wreck decides to start falling off and heading down. You and I know it's going to take along with it everything. I'm talking radios, plywood, most of the burial mound and any of us that are close enough to get sucked along. It's a deathtrap."

"I'll do it," said a young black man, taking off his fire coat as he came forward.

Sammy said, "Billy. Your mother and father would kill me if I let you do this."

"It's my decision, not theirs."

Sammy put his arm around the volunteer. "I know that."

Billy said, "I haven't got a wife and kids. Let me do my job, Chief."

Billy stood there, rain lacing his face, his eyes bright. "Bobby's got to be pulled out of there, doesn't he? No different than a bad fire. Besides, the kid's grandfather risked his life for us. Least a River Sunday fireman can do is pay him back."

Sammy shook his head. "Get your gear," he said.

"Right, Chief," said Billy.

"I'm not sure they'll have time to use that thing," said Pete, looking at the emergency air tank. Charlie had fixed up a radio for the volunteer to strap to his head as he went down. One of the all-weather suits in the equipment that Sammy had brought over from shore was adapted for the volunteers to wear. It would be useful in keeping a volunteer as smooth as possible against the mud. For the digging itself, Mudman had come up with a simple carry bag which held a small shovel and several precut two by four pine studs for shoring the tunnel ceiling and sides. The bag, which would hang down beside the worker as he was suspended, could be used for material that had to be removed. The earth that could not be pushed ahead in the hole or compacted against the walls could be put into the bag for retrieval when the worker returned to the surface. Two flashlights were hung around the volunteer's neck so they pointed ahead as he descended. A small air tank and mask for emergencies was strapped to the volunteer's chest.

"Better to have it than not," said Sammy.

Finally Billy was ready, dressed in his gear, kneeling on the plywood next to Cathy and Richard.

Mudman asked him, "Are you sure you got everything?"

"We'll find out," said Billy. "Get it done," and he gave the thumb's up.

Billy was first hoisted by his harness so that he was head down against the mud. He moved his arms in front of his chest and began immediately to dig into the ground. Being the first, he had to enlarge the entry hole, which was only a few inches in diameter. He dug for a while, piling muck beside him. Cathy and Richard then pushed the excavated material to the edge of the plywood. After a few minutes they had created a large pile and had started a second. The rain quickly turned the earth to liquid and it dribbled out on the mound surface away from the hole. Mudman eased the taut line to the harness and allowed Billy to drop into the ground. Soon Billy's head and shoulders were down under the surface and eventually only his rubber boots stuck up from the edge. He was essentially suspended in the dig. To get out, he would have to rely on Mudman and the others.

Billy's voice came over the loudspeaker. "I'm going downward on a slant of about twenty or thirty degrees. The hole itself is about six inches in diameter ahead of me, a little wider than it is tall. Ahead is a twist where the animals have headed in another direction and made it wider. I am digging it out carefully, taking off only the material I need so that I can squeeze through."

"Any sign of muskrats?" asked Mudman.

"I see a lot of tracks on the tunnel floor, for sure," chuckled Billy. "I keep the light shining in front of me. Every once in a while and maybe far ahead I might see a glint of some eyes, but it's hard to tell. I'm sure they aren't happy to see me coming into their living room."

"Any sign of what went wrong with the microphone?" asked Charlie.

"No. It's running alongside of me and I can't see any damage to the wire."

Mudman interrupted, "You've gone in about five feet. We can barely see your boots. Don't get careless. It's time to set up one of those roof supports like I showed you, Billy."

"I'd rather wait a bit until I get a few more inches into the mound."

"Don't take any chances."

A blast of rain tore at the radio tent. Hank asked, "What's the latest on the weather?"

"Storm is right on time," said Charlie, adjusting his earphones. "We've got less than an hour before the surge makes the water too high. About midnight I'd guess."

In front of Hank, out in the swamp, the glare from the large spotlights at the mound bounced over the whitecaps of the swells. He hit his fist into his palm in frustration.

"Everything takes time," said Pete, seeing how upset Hank was.

"A lot of good going for that tractor did us," said Hank.

Sammy said, "We wouldn't have known if we hadn't tried. Besides, the tractor did find the airplane; helped us get an idea where it was. You can't say that wasn't good, Hank."

"Don't you worry none," said Mudman. "This is going to work, you'll see."

"OK," came Billy's voice. "I got a little earth falling from the roof. I'm going to put up one of your braces, Mudman."

"Take the long pieces, one on bottom and one on the top. Put the two short timbers to hold them out," said Mudman.

Billy answered, his voice squealing in the speaker, "I'm trying to get the wood in place. I can see the wire going ahead of me into the hole."

Mudman checked the block and tackle. The rope was taut against the supporting timbers and extended to a stake at Mudman's feet where the end was secured.

Hank tapped the microphone. "Too much time. Billy should have reported by now."

Mudman looked at Hank. "We can get him out pretty quick."

Charlie spoke into the microphone. "Billy, come on back."

They heard only the background static.

Pete looked over in concern. "Something's happened."

Sammy put another sandbag on the wall. "We better get him up."

Mudman and Hank were already pulling on the exit rope.

"I can see his boots, but there's no movement," Sammy called out. Sammy punched numbers into his cell phone, calling for a boat from shore with paramedics aboard. "We should have had those guys out here standing by," he muttered.

Mudman swept the rainwater off his face. "The mud got him. We didn't count on all this rain coming down. The rain has entered the hole and caused walls to collapse around him," he said.

Billy came up, suspended in the air by his waist, his head down.

"He's breathing," said Sammy, cleaning Billy's unconscious face, as the others took off Billy's digging apparatus.

Sammy's face clouded. "That's it. I'm not sending down any more of my people."

Mudman said, "Wind keeps on picking up and next time the hole will be filled even quicker. It's getting very dangerous. The next person might not get out."

Chapter Nineteen

Melissa came up then, Cincy beside her, and said to Mudman, "I'm going down next. I want to get my son."

Pete tried to tell her how dangerous it was but she refused to listen. Hank himself stood back, realizing that this was the General's granddaughter, matured into a woman used to having her way, seeing her as a Mrs. Pond in the making. Like the others at the mound, he was able only to watch her, astonished as the rest of them, as she pulled herself into the suit left behind as Billy was taken down to the boats. She pulled the bag of support timbers up over her shoulder. Then, before they knew it, she had hooked the rope to her harness.

Mudman, with Hank's reluctant assistance, lifted her upside down until she was poised over the hole. Then she moved into the opening head first, pulling herself down with her hands grabbing into the space that Billy had constructed. The two men, standing in the walkway behind the tripod, eased the rope as she descended, letting out slack as she required on her radio contacts.

"We'll put a tarp over the hole after you get down," radioed Mudman.

"That might keep the rain out for a while," she answered, her voice clear and determined.

Pete handed up a square of canvas cloth to Cathy and Richard so they could spread it to protect the opening. The cloth was snugged as close as possible to the descent rope.

"I repeat, send one of the paramedics out here," said Sammy, talking into his hand held. Then he clicked off the phone and swore.

Melissa called up, "The tunnel Billy made is still here down to about nine feet. My face is against some fallen earth but it's easy to move out of the way. I'm making up the roof support here before I go ahead."

"You've got another ten feet at least before you get close to the airplane," replied Mudman.

"Might be she'll miss it altogether. All this shifting of the fuselage," observed Sammy.

"I'm starting to fill my bag," she said.

In his mind, he saw flash portraits of Melissa as she used to be, in her cut off shorts, sandals, and simple red halter, long hair and sunglasses, holding her can of Doctor Pepper. His mind moved to remembering the touch of her tanned bare body as they lay together on the green grass behind the General's mansion.

He remembered the old warrior, too. The General's local exploits were more important to the citizens anyway. When the General arrived in River Sunday during the Depression, he immediately employed a dozen men rebuilding the oldest of the then deserted tobacco mansions along the Nanticoke River near River Sunday. The house had been lived in by the only remaining descendent of the building family, a woman who had been deported to Richmond during the Civil War. She returned and lived alone there for many years. She was insane according to legend. Stories had it that she walked at night on the overgrown lawn, her white hair down to her waist, dressed in a tattered red and white dress. She would toss candles a few yards and let them sputter out in the darkness.

Hank, as he stood in the rain, was getting worried. He had not heard Melissa's voice on the radio for a while.

His reverie continued. During the fifty years after she died what was left of the mansion became overgrown with vines and its walls, filled with animals, were about to fall down. The General bought the place and all its barns for unpaid taxes which was another windfall for the town. He fixed it up and proceeded to have the best parties, perhaps the only parties, the area had seen since before the Depression. The new settlers in River Sunday, that is, the ones who had money, and the still living albeit mostly broke of the older colonials like the Allinghams went to call, drink his whiskey, and praise the General but mostly perhaps for the quality of his whiskey. The General, who was never a fool, enjoyed the respect that his money brought and probably gave Melissa the idea that she could only get this same kind of adulation by spending money. The problem was that the General lived in such a depressed time that very little money could buy a great deal of respect. He did it in such an offhand way that he never took himself into a stratified level of local society. Everyone felt welcome at his house even if most people were not actually invited.

Melissa, unfortunately, came along in a more prosperous time. She never understood the reason for her grandfather's social success and acceptance - that his seemingly endless bounty was welcome in a time of misfortune. It made him a savior, one of their own, and a stability on which the people could depend. The General was the welfare state country squire of River Sunday and it boded him well during his lifetime.

Melissa tried to follow in his footsteps, to codify his success, and failed miserably. Her invitation lists were noticeably shallow, bereft of the true citizens of the town and notable for their inclusion of only the very wealthy. Her former childhood friends felt out of place and finally unwelcome.

Hank was one of those.

Hank moved closer to the hole and watched the rope trembling with Melissa's descent. She had not been lucky with parents. Not like he had been.

Melissa's mother, one of the father's sailboat girlfriends, lived in Baltimore on a healthy allowance and scarcely came to River Sunday except, as Hank understood from Melissa, when she had to pick up her check. After the father died Hank never saw her again and she never expressed any desire to see him. Melissa asked her to come to their wedding but the woman claimed a bout of arthritis and that she was not well enough to make the trip across the Chesapeake Bay.

-John lost at sea today-stop-Fell off yacht-stop-Unable to rescue in seas-stop-Condolences to family-stop-Yacht being shipped back to New York next freighter deck space available-stop-Thank you-stop-

Hank asked the General why the words "thank you" were in the telegram. The old man, sitting back in his leather den chair, a stuffed Canada goose on the wall over him, his fresh whiskey in hand, stared at Hank without a tear in his eyes. He finally said gruffly that maybe it was sent by the crew of the boat his son was racing against.

He thought back to the warnings he had about marrying Melissa.

The General knew it right then about his daughter. He told Hank, "You know, boy, you and Melissa get married that's all fine but you got to keep up with her, boy, because this little lady is going to step out on you someday. She doesn't even recognize yet what she can do and one day she's going to go after whatever she wants on her own and you got to be ready to go along, or you are going to get left behind."

The wedding was before all that. The General arranged to have a yacht, a hundred footer, cruise up the Nanticoke River as far as the inlet creek around the north end of the Wilderness. The big cruiser had a captain and a two women crew. When Hank and Melissa went aboard they were waited on completely. The boat cruised the Chesapeake down to Norfolk and back up to the Delaware canal, stopping at the small towns and sometimes just anchored in little rivers and creeks.

He came back to the present and yelled at Charlie. "Call her!"

Melissa replied immediately. "I'm working on getting more earth into the bag. It's cramped here. Everything takes time. The wall is about three inches in front of my face. The flashlight illuminates a small part of it. The rest I find by my fingers."

In a few minutes she called again. "I want to roll over and lie on my back to rest but I am afraid that the roof will fall in if I do."

"Melissa," said Mudman. "You're very brave. Take it easy though."

Melissa radioed that she noticed a root sticking through in the corner of the tunnel ahead. She cleared dirt and moved closer to the spot. With her right hand she grasped a part of the wet wood and tried to move it. It gave a little and a chunk of earth fell down ahead of her into the rat tunnel.

"I think I can work around this root," she said, her voice showing exhaustion. "It's holding me back."

"We could get a line around it and pull from up here," suggested Mudman.

"If you do that it might bring the whole tunnel down on me. I'll have to do it from here. I'm going to reinforce this section though before I proceed. I'm putting up the two by fours."

Then another report came. "Hey, we got a surprise here. It just fell away, the root when I was tapping in the boards. There's a larger hole opened up ahead of me. I'm trying to see with the flashlight."

In a few moments she reported again. "Ha. I know where that squealing was coming from. We got ourselves a whole nest of the little rascals down here."

"Tell us about it," said Mudman. Hank remembered what Duke had said about the muskrats coming out of the mound.

"I can just make out their heads," she said.

"Bobby said animals were around him."

"I can't see down too far into the hole. Right below the hole turns again and the flashlight won't light around the corner. I can head on further down."

"Can you get by the animals?"

"It's like they are on a ledge just below me, maybe two or three feet."

"All right, we're going to pay out some more line," said Mudman.

"I'm moving down," said Melissa.

Suddenly, screams came through the loudspeakers and rippled across the swamp.

Hank heart lurched.

Mudman called frantically on the radio.

Melissa gasped her reply amid her screams, "Good God, pull me out. Pull me out."

"Tell us what happened. We're pulling," yelled Mudman.

"Rats are tearing at my face. I'm hitting at them with the flashlight. Damnit. The light went out." Melissa's screams interrupted her words. Then she said, "I can't see them. Pull me out. Oh God, Hank. Mudman, pull me out."

Hank was on the plywood as she came out of the hole. Her face was covered with small cuts that were bleeding down on her coverall. He took her by the waist and laid her carefully on the wood. She was whimpering.

From the walkway several yards away, Cincy, standing in her oversize windbreaker, was calling. "Hank, is she all right?"

"I don't know, Cincy."

Hank carried her to the boat where he set her out in a stretcher laid out in the bottom. Cincy bent over her, trying to wipe away some of the blood from the animal bite wounds on Melissa's face. Melissa was moaning, trying to move her hand to her face.

"You're going to be all right," whispered Hank.

Melissa grasped at his hand.

Meanwhile, at the other end of the mound, Will was working by himself as if he were in a daze and unaware of the catastrophic storm. The last time they checked on him, his tractor was up to its axles in marsh water. He was still digging at a small tunnel he had made where the trench had been. Around him were fallen sandbags and water. In the rain, the remaining walls of the old trench were slippery and very weak. With the rising water, they would soon tumble inward. Will, however, worked steadily and intently, not concerned about the danger he was in, resisting stubbornly and forcefully any attempt by anyone to get him to move to safety.

Will stood up in the rain, moving dirt off his face with his left hand. He used the shovel he had in his right hand as a walking stick and steadied himself, his eyes on the ground ahead of him.

Then he suddenly called out, "Pete, are you still there?"

Hank heard Pete answer, "Hey there, Will, you about ready to give up on your digging?"

"I can't give up. I'm too close to finding that rudder. I could use some help. I need just a man or two to help me dig."

"Will, there's only a few volunteers still here. We don't have enough to handle what we are doing."

"You still think Bobby is alive, Pete?" he called over the wind shrieks.

Melissa heard Will from where she lay in mud next to the mound. She whispered to Hank, "Why can't he understand? Why can't he help Bobby?"

Will snapped, "Pete, you got to get me some men."

Pete shook his head. "Can't do that, Will."

"You and Sammy. You can do it."

"Will, I can't free up any of the rescue team," said Sammy.

"Remember you wanted me to talk to some of the board of trustees at the Allingham School. They are rich folks. They can give money for your fire volunteers. I can talk to them. You want some money for a new station. I'll talk to them."

Sammy shouted at Will. "Nobody wants your money."

"I'll give you some of the money I make from the land. I'll give it to you directly. Forget the Fire Department. Use it for a vacation."

Pete turned to Hank. "He's alone. That's the worst a man can be. He's alone when he's in trouble and needs others."

Hank thought back to the bullying child Will had been. All his true personality was coming out. Nothing was left out in that mud of the quiet schoolteacher, the gentleman of River Sunday who had walked the main streets, full of strength, his head high.

An old story came to mind. One Shot Will. That name started around town when one Sunday afternoon a farmer found Will and Melissa in the act. Hank would have just put on his clothes.

Not Will. He tried to get the farmer to forget what he saw. He was standing there naked as a jaybird, arguing with a middle-aged farmer. The farmer tried to keep from snickering at what the preachers call a backslider and a ridiculous one at that. Melissa was behind the corn, drunk and not able to remember in which corn row she had left her blue jeans. Melissa yelled for him to get dressed.

Instead Will kept on talking to that poor man. He followed the farmer right back over to his barn, still naked. He did not want the farmer to tell what he had seen. At the barn was the man's wife and little boy sitting in the shade. That's when the farmer picked up a board and threatened Will off his land.

Hank knew about the whole episode within a few hours. From that day on, people referred to Will Allingham as "One Shot Will." Even the girls and boys at his school would taunt him by scrawling the nickname on bathroom walls.

Melissa opened her eyes. "That letter, Hank. He needs to talk to you about it. I've been so wrong," she said, and gripped his hand tighter. "I lost my father to the water," she said. "I didn't want to lose Bobby the same way."

The General had told Hank long ago about Melissa's father. Hank knew the truth. Her father had jumped without a lifebelt and none of his crew could turn the boat around to get back to him in time. Melissa was never told.

Hank suspected she knew that her father was a weak man, likely a suicide.

Melissa said, "I thought a lot about my father and me when I was down there. I want Bobby to know we love him, to know we'd risk our lives for him." Her free hand touched her puffed face. "I wanted that for him."

"He knows that," Hank said, softly. "You proved a lot going down in the hole."

Sammy said, "We got to get her to shore."

Melissa sat up, moving her arms up and down, her eyes like glass.

"She's delirious," said a volunteer.

"You think I'm Judas, don't you, Hank?" asked Melissa.

"We'll give her something when we get her to shore," the fireman said to Hank.

Melissa leaned her head back in exhaustion and murmured, "It's all over though, Hank. You don't have to try to save him down in that tunnel. You'll die down there. I don't want to lose you, too. Bobby's dead. I know that."

Hank watched Mudman fastening the descent harness on his legs. Then, Hank said loud enough so she could hear him over the screaming wind, "No, we are not giving up, Melissa."

As Hank got back to the others, Pete was talking to Sammy outside the tent.

"We've got to get those animals out of the way."

"I can handle it," said Hank.

"We'll have to kill them," said Mudman.

"No," came a voice from the other end of the mound.

They all turned to see the long row boat which had just touched against the shoreline. A shadowy figure at the back leaned down to turn off his outboard motor.

Pete said, "Jimmy."

Jimmy Swift stood up from his seat and gracefully walked forward in the tipsy boat, then jumped to the sandbags. He moved along the walkway, stepping around the collapsed bags, steadily coming toward Hank.

When he was close, he said, in the soft knowledgeable voice that Hank and Pete knew so well, "I'm sorry for your boy, Mr. Hank."

Hank nodded.

Cincy came up to him and embraced him. "The muskrats, Jimmy. Melissa was badly hurt."

"I know of this," said Jimmy.

"I realize that for sure. Help us," said Cincy.

Jimmy closed his eyes and moved his lips.

Hank saw the plywood surrounding the hole out in the top of the mound. He saw the two children perched on the boards, still there, their hands ready to help guide Mudman in his harness down into the earth.

"Stand back," Jimmy said out loud. Then, his slicker glistening from the rain, he held up his hands and moved his lips again, the rain coming down the sides of his head.

Cathy called out, "The muskrats are coming out."

"The little critters," said Mudman.

From the hole, muskrats of all sizes had popped up, their eyes bright spots in the darkness. One by one they scrambled out of the hole and across the plywood. Cathy and Richard stood back at the edge of the plywood, eyes wide open.

"Like they're in a trance," said Cathy.

"Yes," said Cincy.

The animals tumbled down and gathered in the downpour beside Jimmy. He started toward his boat, the muskrats falling in behind him, their paws stepping in cadence with the silent Native American.

Jimmy put a small plank against the side of his rowboat. The muskrats in single file climbed it and jumped into the boat, assembling as a furry, squirming mass. Jimmy waded in water to his knees, holding the side of the boat until all the rats were aboard. Then he clambered in, started the motor, and slowly backed the boat away. A final animal had appeared on the walkway, separating itself from the others and staying behind.

"Cochise," said Cathy.

"So it was his nest after all," said Pete. "He was going down there to take care of them."

"He wanted to attract us to the hole so we would help," Cathy corrected.

Sammy picked up the harness.

"Mudman, you ready to go down?"

Chapter Twenty

Hank handled the rope for Mudman's descent. As his friend disappeared in the hole, he listened for the first message. The radio static sounded sharply against the downpour and the shouts of the remaining firemen working with Sammy.

He remembered another time when the roles had been reversed, and Mudman had been security to him, had been holding on to him. Mudman had saved his life, as well as his sanity. They had run to the shelter in the darkness, the explosions going off around them from the incoming mortars. In the back of the shelter, deep among the assembled soldiers, the priest was praying. One of the soldiers had a pocket radio and it picked up part of a song on Armed Forces Radio. The stanzas interrupted the prayers, and the sound was further punctuated as the men choked and coughed in the dust-laden heat. The song was about seeing the green grass of home.

Another blast, closer outside the shelter, disrupted the rest of the music and prayers with its thunder. Mudman stood beside him. He began whispering in Hank's ear, speaking slowly, bending his face down under the lip of Hank's helmet so Hank could hear every word, even with the punctuating explosions. He told Hank he was not a coward, that he was sick, unable to stop shaking from the fear of being closed in, of being buried. Mudman said, "You hear that song? Think about the green grass outside." He had gone on, "Think about the green grass, buddy, think of the blades of grass, millions of them like the baseball or football field at the high school in River Sunday."

Hank's mind had remembered Melissa in the grass behind the General's mansion. He had smelled the scent of her body.

Mudman had continued whispering, "Charlie's out there in the night, one of him for each one of them mortar rounds, Hank. He's brought his round all the way from North Vietnam, all the way just to shoot it this night. Just after you hear the incoming, Hank, you think about him running, running fast as he can to get to cover. You smile, Hank, because you know what is coming and you don't want to be that Charley. His life is over because he has to run as fast as he can out of that rice paddy before the bullets get him."

Mudman had gone on whispering, "Puff the magic dragon is up there and pretty soon you'll hear it, Hank."

"Puff," Hank had replied. He had forgotten about Puff.

"Puff can knock out every blade of green grass in that field with his burst of machine gun fire. Hank, just think of that. Charlie Cong is running and he isn't going to get away."

Then Hank had heard the noise of the propeller-driven cargo plane above them, the noise of the airborne Gatling gun, the noise like a contractor cutting through the concrete of a street with a pneumatic hammer, the steady eerie sound.

Mudman had whispered, "Think about Charlie dying, Hank, not you. He is afraid, Hank, not you. He can't escape because he is chewed up like green grass."

Mudman's voice blared over the loudspeakers, shaking Hank out of his memories. "Hank, keep that rope tight," said Mudman. He began to describe the shape of the tunnel. He said the walls of the hole were very wet and water was dripping. The water under the mound was approaching the level of the water in the swamp. The muskrat tunnels were flooding, bringing tidewater into the mound and Mudman was descending down into this flood.

Pete spoke up. "Fifteen feet," he said, reading Hank's mind.

Hank nodded. Pete meant that the top of the mound normally was about fifteen feet above the level of the swamp water at a high tide. The rest of the island was sodden at most high tides, fairly dry at low tides. With the water at the edge of the sandbags, the water table in the mound must be rising even higher. Certainly any part of the airplane that was below fifteen feet from the top of the mound would be under water soon, and if they didn't get Bobby out of there, then he'd be dead.

Mudman reported that his sack of dirt was almost full and that he would bring it up to empty it. Then he planned, he said, to come down again.

Hank prepared to start hauling the rope upward.

There was a jerk.

The rope stopped moving.

"Boys, I'm in trouble." said Mudman. His voice sounded worried, not the normal casual Mudman.

"What happened, Mudman? Come on back," radioed Hank.

"Broke my arm, I think. Hurts like hell."

"We'll get you out," said Hank.

Mudman continued, his voice shrill with pain. "I put the ceiling beam into place. I hit the damn board too hard and it went back into the mound. I think I have broken into another tunnel beside this one."

"Just let the rope pull you up."

"Board came down on me. I was completely covered up, right to my eyeballs. I've got on the air tank but so much muck around me, I can't use it."

"A little bit more. I can see your boots." Hank was at the hole.

"That was my good arm."

"We're going to pull you out."

"I'm sure as hell sorry, Hank."

Hank had Mudman's boots in his hands. His friend was halfway out of the ground.

"Goddamn," said his old friend as he tried to grin, his face upside down.

"You got that right," Hank answered, the rain biting his face.

"It's up to you," said Mudman, breathing hard.

"We're going to get you into shore to fix that arm," said Sammy.

"No," said Mudman. "I'm broken but I ain't going anywhere. I'll stay here, Hank."

Chapter Twenty-One

Around him he smelled the odor of wet animal fur mixed with the stink of swamp water. The tiny opening above him, the oval of light from the rescue team against the night sky, disappeared. The dim glare got less as he went deeper. He felt a trickle of fear but only a little. He crawled into the corridor, the flashlight showing little more than four walls of a rectangle. The blood flowed into his upside down head. He felt slightly dizzy but he handled this. He remembered standing on his hands to entertain Bobby when the boy was a baby. He touched the walls of the opening, not much wider or higher than his body. He kept inching forward on the downward slant of the passage, knowing he neared his son.

Captain Steele's voice crackled on the radio. "The storm surge is raising the water level."

"We only have time for this trip," replied Hank into the microphone attached to the side of his head.

"I'm giving you some more slack," said Mudman.

Hank reached the end of the previous dig. Here a small, almost round hole appeared - the tunnel that the muskrats used. Mudman had made his last cuts in the walls before the timbers had crashed down. Carefully Hank repaired the structure and, after testing the boards, began to scrape away new soil.

Even with the thoughts of Bobby, the fear quickly came over him. He imagined the walls moving and squeezing him. His arms and legs refused to move.

"Why am I so afraid?" he reasoned with himself. He thought of his son.

"Bobby will make me succeed," he proclaimed, as if his son were a god who granted power. He heard again, deep in memory, the screams of his father's fear in closed spaces. The images rushed through his mind as he lay there, shovel in hand, afraid to move.

Long ago, on a day when he was eight or nine years old, he was going to the basement to check the daily laundry for his mother. He didn't like descending into the dark cellar lit by a single light hanging from an electric cord. As he walked down the crude wooden stairs his father had built he smelled the bleach in wet laundry.

"Dad," he called.

"Here," his father answered. He had a strong manly voice, a commanding sound. "You helping Mommy?"

"Yessir," Hank replied.

His father answered, his voice strangely strangled as if he had a rope around his neck. "I'm getting a few bulbs for the greenhouse. I remembered I put them down here last fall."

His mother was vacuuming a rug in their living room above the store.

The cellar light went out

Hank said, "Mom's blown the fuse again."

Two quick crashes followed; heavy things falling upstairs.

In the dark, the plant bulbs fell from his father's hands, tumbling softly as they hit the concrete floor. His father thumped first to his knees then outstretched on the floor, groaning.

Hank descended toward the older man, his own legs weakening. When he reached his father, there was enough glimmer from the basement windows to see the man. He had fallen flat on the old cracked cement, his face buried in his arms, the position of a person who was trying to penetrate, to hide deep in the stone.

His father whispered, "Why don't they stop?"

"Who's they? Mommy blew a fuse and then she dropped something." Hank kneeled at his side, pulling at his father. "Daddy?"

The man pressed deeper into the floor.

Hank stood up, thinking he should call upstairs.

His father turned on his side and stared at Hank, eyes wet, face red. "I'll get up."

Hank's mother yelled from upstairs. "Hank. Hope I didn't scare you. I dropped a couple of your father's books."

"OK, Mom."

Hank stared at his father.

His father said, "We have to fix the fuse."

Hank tried to help.

His father waved him off. "I can stand."

They moved slowly, holding each other. Hank's unreasoning fear of the walls started that day. He began trembling in all tight rooms and closed places.

The wet tunnel soil brought him to the present. He thought of the risks taken by his friends on the mound above. He felt shame.

His thoughts raced. That's a testament to love and to a great child. It's all being thrown away by me, frozen here in this tunnel. Soon they'll realize I'm terrified down here. I realize I don't care about Bobby. Melissa was right to take him away from me.

He panicked. He knew he had to escape. Nothing else mattered. If he escaped he welcomed being a coward for the rest of his life. Anything, only let him get away from this tube of imprisoning earth.

Hank ripped at the walls, trying to make more space. He tried to turn from his downward position. His hands grabbed at the slope until his body squeezed half way upward. He clambered toward the surface.

"Hank," the radio blared. "The rope's gone slack. Answer back. Are you all right?"

All right? How about the fear of dying, the fear of being buried? The walls of his grave.

He talked to himself, a murmur. "Father Tom told me that none of us can escape the walls around us. Oh, Jesus, even the Earth is hemmed by its air and the universe. You are in your body, a form of spacesuit, in the middle of eternal universe. You are damn well going to be closed in by your grave and the hereafter too. You got no escape. Running away from closed spaces is never possible. You have to teach yourself and then you'll be all right."

Mudman spoke, his voice distant, "Talk to me, Hank."

The trembling stopped. Hank smelled the stink. He felt water on his knees. He could see it trickling from the side of the muskrat hole below him.

He stopped thrashing against the walls of the hole. Wet air touched his skin. He wiped the caked earth from his face.

Hank realized that his son must be even more afraid, with puddles up his waist if not higher. He might be keeping only his head above in some corner of the aircraft. He kept wishing to hear Bobby one more time.

"I'm making progress," Hank reported, his voice steadier.

Hank went back to work. He turned and made almost a foot of new depth in following the muskrat tunnel.

The line became taut.

Pete spoke into the microphone. "Worried about you." The old man did not ask Hank any more.

Hank reached to his left side to add dug earth to his bag. As he did he pushed on the wall hard for balance. His elbow sank into the muck and the earth collapsed. Gritty mire sucked against his face.

He froze, thinking fast, so as to not make the situation worse.

"I'm in a little bit of trouble," he called in.

"Talk to us," came back Mudman.

"Sinking into the mound."

"More line?" said Mudman.

"No, for God's sake, no. I'll fall deeper. Steady until I get myself back on track."

Hank decided to build one of Mudman's frames and to pray the tunnel held the weight. The bottom tended to be firmer than the ceiling and sides.

"What's happening?" called Mudman on the radio.

"I'm trying to get myself on something solid."

As he dug, a clod of earth fell on his head causing sudden pain. He reached up and pushed it away. He looked at the clod. Something was strange about it. He scraped at the mud. A light color appeared against the mud. He stared at it.

It was a skull. "One of the old Nanticoke heros," he mumbled. As he stared at the bone, he noticed the space for the left eye. It was not circular. Instead it was elongated top and bottom with a broken cleft. He knew. He grunted, "This guy was a hero all right. He got a spear right in the eye. Wonder if he was a good hero or an evil hero. What side was he on?"

Hank worked fast. Every movement caused more pain in his back because of his position, hanging suspended and lifting his arms over his head to work. He stretched every muscle beyond capacity. First he placed the base board of the frame. This two by four was three feet long. He stuck it as solidly into the base of the tunnel as he could. Next went the two short side parts jammed on the first wood. The next step was to set the top. Here he had more trouble because he had to clear the earth which had fallen against his right shoulder and face.

After a few minutes of slow and careful work he had all in place. It went slowly, requiring him to tap it into a squared position against the other pieces. He tested the boards and they seemed secure and tight. He had to rest, his chin into the muck.

"I have the brace. Proceeding." He felt waves of nausea. He had been able to forget terror which stayed in his brain, lurking below his resolve. He kept going, weak.

"It's bad, Mudman," he said slowly.

"We better get you out."

"No. Not yet." Yet he understood he was risking their lives, too.

"Hank, tell us about the water coming in," asked Pete.

"Lots coming through the wall."

"How wide ahead?" asked Sammy. His voice seemed weaker, as though the Chief himself had lost energy and resolve.

"Slope turning down ahead of me."

Hank heard some static. "More line," said Mudman. "Keep it straight so we can pull you out."

"How in the hell can I tangle? Line is all above me."

Mudman chuckled, "Keeping you alert."

Hank moved the light. Then the line stopped moving.

"What's the matter?"

"We got an emergency."

"What?"

No answer.

He hung in the air, the dank smell irritating his nostrils. Then his flashlight went dead.

"Birdy Pond capsized her boat, overloaded with sandbags for us."

"Is she all right?"

"She's more upset she lost her hat. Bob Johnny is out trying to bail her."

Hank thought about Bobby again. The boy had asked the priest one Sunday, "How do I think about death?"

"As you get older, you will teach yourself," Father Tom answered. Hank remembered that Bobby thought the priest was making a joke.

The line loosened, then tightened, jerking him.

"What's happening?" Hank called.

"The block slipped on the post," replied Mudman.

Hank tapped the flashlight again and it went on this time. As his eyes became used to the new light, he scanned beneath him.

Ahead, a glint reflected, guiding him like a pinpoint star.

Chapter Twenty-Two

"I've located the microphone about six feet ahead," Hank radioed back

"You must be close," answered Mudman.

Hank continued to crawl. The hole became as wide as the rectangular opening that Hank had been cutting.

"Bigger up ahead." His eyes followed the communication wire into the darkness. He spotted the instrument covered with Charlie's grey tape. He trained his flashlight on the area. Beyond was a small cavern with a mud-covered rounded shape.

He was sure. "I've found the plane," he yelled. "The wreck curves away from me on my left. I'm on the starboard side of the wreck."

Metal glared where muck had scraped off. The round shape extended upward from where Hank's flash touched. The cylinder was heavily encrusted on most of its surface and hard to distinguish from the rest of the earth. Also, he noted the fuselage rested half in water. The water rippled advising Hank it was filling the space fast.

Cheers sounded on his radio.

"We're putting the Captain on."

Hank had to get closer to the airplane. "Let me have more line, Pete."

The Captain spoke. "Be careful as you approach. Tell me what's ahead and I can help you get into the cockpit area."

Hank reported that the small cavern ended. Part of the cockpit extended huge to his front and above him. Fresh wet mud scrapes on the metal indicated the plane had just moved slightly. He figured the muskrat tunnel had originally been closer to the nose of the aircraft.

"Describe how she sits."

"Nose down, about two or three feet."

"You do this wrong and you and the boy go down."

"I understand. I'm trying to grip the earth."

He maneuvered slowly. He was moving horizontally trying to keep his weight on the mud. As he got to the muck against the metal fuselage, his face was only inches from the curve. To his left, the light shone on a small clean portion of the hull. He made careful progress. He had to open up a path for his body, pulling and clearing mire as he created space to crawl.

"Give me more."

The line lurched about twelve inches.

"Bobby said he had water inside," said Pete from above.

"The water's mostly below me. I'm further up the side of the plane. Wait, I see something else," said Hank.

"What?"

"The light we sent down to him. It's tangled in part of the wing. The section is buckled and bent backwards."

"What's above you?" asked the Captain.

"I've got some blue fuselage paint here," said Hank.

"Good," said the Captain. "She may not be too corroded."

"I'm continuing ahead."

Hank stared up the round hull shape. The latticework frame of the canopy area appeared.

"I'm going toward the glass now."

"The earth is probably mashed in front of the glass."

"Wait a minute. A noise."

He realized what he was hearing. Dripping water inside the hollow fuselage hit like small projectiles against the metal.

"I'm going to tap on the hull."

He touched the airplane lightly. Two taps.

"Good idea," said the Captain.

Hank tapped. He waited.

"Has he answered?"

"Quiet so far."

Two distinct return taps sounded. He answered.

Three taps came from inside the fuselage.

"He answered me," Hank yelled into the microphone. "He's here. My God. Tell everyone. He's alive."

"Get to him, Hank."

He worked, moving upward. In front of him pieces of flat glass appeared with the surrounding bars of metal, the muntins. His face was close to the panes, not more than six inches away. He cleaned the two large panes along the length of the canopy. Above it was solid muck. The glass on this side of the airplane had to work. He had no time to get to the other side. Digging would take too long.

"Like a window," he reported.

"Right," said the Captain. "The pilot space."

Hank flashed the light.

"I can't see inside the cockpit."

"Probably so filthy with grime," answered the Captain.

The tapping continued and he answered. A small circle began to appear in one of the panes closest to Hank. A small circle of clear panel appeared, perhaps a couple of inches in diameter. Behind the clearing Bobby's fingers and part of his nose pressed.

"Bobby."

"Move the canopy easy," advised the Captain.

"I'm going to try." He pressed but the canopy did not open.

"Locked?" called the Captain.

Hank tried again. His body slipped on the side of the fuselage. Beneath him the airplane shook and slid deeper. He tried to keep his own weight from pushing against the metal.

"What happened?" Mudman called. "The rope went taut again."

"Slipping."

"How much?"

"About a foot."

"What did you do?"

"I fell against it trying to open the canopy."

He could not hold on and slipped down the side of the hull. Then his left foot hit what must have been part of the broken wing. He grabbed at the muck behind him as he began to pull himself up again. Trying once again to keep his weight mostly on the mud, he crawled carefully to where his face was near the squares.

"I'm by the window. Bobby's finger is on the inside of the glass."

The Captain said, "Hank. Don't try anything. I'm going to find out about the canopy."

Hank waited in the darkness. A mistake would send Bobby moving away too fast to stop. He prayed the boy had not been hit as the plane shifted. He watched the boy's silent trapped fingers moving slowly in circles inside the small clear section of panel.

"Hank, this is Captain Steele."

"Go ahead."

"We've come to some conclusions, Hank. First off, Bobby has air because the pilot did not open the top. That fact has saved his life so far."

The Captain continued, "Air inside is giving pressure against the earth so the fuselage keeps its form. We got a problem. When we release to get him out, the plane will lose the air pressure which keeps the water from filling the compartment. If we don't get him out right away he'll drown."

He went on, "We think because of the corrosion the latch is not going to open. No use to try. We've been talking and we got a way for you break into the cockpit. From the manual here's how to clear those panes from the outside."

"Read it."

"Remove the red cover plate at the lower edge of the canopy on either side and pull out the exposed handle. Pull out the partition between the two panes by means of the ring located at its lower end. Pull out the panes."

He added, "If the metal is not too corroded and if we are very lucky, you should be able to open a mullion partition."

"How much time do we have?"

"The air inside the canopy should last long enough for you get Bobby out. Stay away from weight on the fuselage. Grab him and pull him. We'll do the rest with the rope."

Pete took the microphone and said, "Sandbags are covered with water. We're out of time. They can't stop the surge anymore."

Hank said, "Bobby must be swimming."

"If it gets too wet up here, we're hauling you out. No sense both of you drowning."

Hank ran the flashlight around the hole down below him. "I'm starting. The water along the side of the fuselage has filled in almost a foot in the last ten minutes."

"The space where Bobby is located is probably filling up too. He's a mighty scared boy," said the Captain.

"I'm trying to be careful. I think I feel stronger than I ever had in my life."

Mudman came on the radio, "Old buddy, we going to have this little boy in his school Monday, right on time."

Hank worked to find the tab. He tried to balance with his feet jammed several inches into the soft earth behind him. He hoped the muck would give him support for a few more minutes as he carefully cleaned mud off a piece of red metal.

"I've found the cover plate," he reported. His flashlight dimmed again. "Corroded and hanging open."

The cover broke free in his hand. He put the metal into the pocket of his coverall, thinking it might help with the latch. The airplane shifted slightly. Hank shook and ran the erratic flash back along the fuselage.

"The airplane's moving."

"Remember," said the Captain. "The heavy nose on the P47 is making a trap for Bobby, moving right down into deeper muck."

The water was rising more quickly. Hank anchored his feet in the slop behind him.

"I'm still working on the latch," Hank reported. He pushed inward. He heard two taps. He answered the taps.

"More noise."

"Bobby is still all right."

Hank continued to scrape at the metal. "I'm trying again." He pushed inward. The latch did not move.

"You better hurry up, Hank. The wind is picking up. We'll have to pull you out in a few minutes."

"I'm pressing harder."

"You're taking a big chance, Hank."

"I don't have any choice." He struck with his right fist, sensing the tremble in the rotten structure, feeling weight shifting. One of the panes moved slightly.

"I've got one pane loose." In the cockpit Bobby's fingers pulled at the glass. The fuselage shook.

Hank pressed in about an inch. Bobby clasped around an edge. Foul smelling air and water spit from the crack.

"We'll pull you out, Bobby," he yelled.

Bobby replied, and his voice was the most wonderful sound he had ever heard. "I know, Daddy."

"Hitting again," warned Hank.

The water was up to his knees and lapping below the canopy. The nose dropped as the plane kept moving.

"You're out of time, Hank. We've got to bring you up." The line tightened around his waist.

"Wait," Hank yelled.

Bobby stared at him. Hank pounded the cockpit frame. Nothing happened. He hit again, this time with all his strength, cramped as he was against the earth. The right pane moved inward slightly.

More foul air rushed by Hank's face.

"Help me," said Bobby through the small crack.

"Hang on, Bobby."

"Daddy."

"Bobby, you pull and I'll push."

"I'm ready."

"Have you got something you can get on top of to boost yourself out?"

"I'm standing on a shelf."

"Here goes."

As they worked, Hank's right hand moved over the boy's small fingers. The pane flew loose and was lost in the interior darkness. The plane shuddered.

"One of them."

He balanced on his left foot which was still on part of the wing below him, and using his left hand, pushed on another one. It did not move.

"If the glass is loose, try pulling outward, Daddy."

"OK." Hank pulled again on the pane and this time it came out in his left hand.

Bobby moved his head through the small opening. He got his shoulders out.

"I'm stuck."

The plane lurched downward slowly without stopping.

"The water is up to my stomach, Daddy."

"Hank," called Mudman, "Time's up."

"Bobby. I'm going to pull on you real hard and I want you to push outward as hard as you can against that shelf you're standing on."

"OK, Daddy."

The plane was sliding faster. Hank put his right arm on the window opening and placed his left hand under the boy's right shoulder. He pulled. Bobby squirmed with pain. The flashlight stopped and they were in black darkness. The metal under Hank's body began to collapse inward.

"You're moving, Bobby. Hang on." His arm entered the fuselage as the cockpit frame crumpled, window muntins and glass breaking outward. The plane had shifted. He was stretching. His pain was unbearable but he did not let Bobby go.

"Bobby, push hard as you can while I pull you."

Bobby's body came free, slowly at first then like a projectile. Hank moved his right hand to grab Bobby. The boy's waist was cradled in Hank's arms, his feet still in the cockpit.

"OK, kid, keep pushing with your feet against the frame. "

He hollered into the radio, "You guys upstairs, pull like hell."

"Roger," said the Captain. The rope tightened and Hank moved backward. The after section of the plane travelled past.

"Bobby, hold tight to me."

The flashlight dropped into the water. Hank saw the light flashing on and off below him, then getting smaller and disappearing as it was sucked down. The airplane creaked into the deeper mire.

"Keep pushing, Bobby."

The child's body slipped away. "Oh God, don't let go, son."

The plane lurched and he lost balance. In the swirl of water, he felt Bobby's right hand grab his legs.

"I'm out, Daddy."

Hank could hear the noise of the aircraft joints creaking, turning into a roar. The heavy engine pulled the plane forward faster and faster, water splashing at them.

"Watch out, Daddy."

Hank ducked as part of the wing section slid by from the earth, turning and bending on itself. A white five-pointed star flashed in front of him, the plane's insignia still on the metal.

Hank was holding Bobby in his feet, the child's head near Hank's knees. Hank was jerked backward, as he came with the rope back through the entrance tunnel. Bobby was above him, both of them going upward upside down, as the hole was falling behind them. He called into the microphone. "Keep pulling us up, for God's sake. Pull us up."

The line continued taut and they moved upward. No sign remained below them in the dark of the muskrat tunnel or the fuselage.

"I see light up ahead," said Bobby, looking up through his legs.

Bobby held Hank's legs with his own hands in a tight grip. Lightning flashed outside. The light glared against the remains of the tunnel below Hank. Hank's mind screamed against the terror overcoming him. The closeness of the tunnel walls was beginning to make his arms weak. Below them water was churning, filling the hole.

"Hold on tight, Bobby, we're almost free, son." Hank fought the weakness. He thought only about the child.

He called up, "You guys speed this up."

Bobby shouted, "Mudman!"

Sammy ordered, "Keep the rope tight."

Bobby screamed, "I'm losing my grip."

Hank tried to sooth his son. "Count with me. Slowly. By twenty we'll be out."

The line dropped suddenly about a foot.

Sammy hollered, "Watch out, you guys. You'll lose them!"

Mudman's voice held tense energy. "The soil gave way for a moment. We're back in business."

The line began moving up again, a few inches at a time but steadily. Bobby's weight was lifted off of him. A strong hand grabbed at Hank's ankles. His head came out of the hole and he felt the rain on his bare skin.

Hank was lowered from the block and tackle down on to the wood. He reached out and hugged his son, who was kneeling beside him. The others worked quickly to undo the harness.

A cheer went up from the volunteers around them.

"No time to celebrate. We got to get out of here," said Pete. One of the plywood sheets was beginning to float in the thin coat of water covering the mound as the water spurted from the muskrat hole.

Sammy shouted, "Come on!" He was holding the lines for a small runabout which was slapping against the soil. The wind spun more of the wood around. Other boats were nearby picking up remaining volunteers and swimming animals.

"Get in." Mudman put Bobby into Sammy's boat and jumped in afterwards. He reached back for Hank. Hank stood up weakly, his hand grasping one of the pine timbers holding the block and tackle.

Sammy called, "Hank, over here!"

The swamp water poured down the large hole like a waterfall.

Sammy's eyes were somber. "You guys been drowned in another minute."

Hank fell into Sammy's boat and was silent, breathing hard, unable to take his eyes from the whirlpool over the muskrat tunnel.

Bobby said, "Thank you, Daddy, for saving my life."

Hank smiled back and used his finger to rub some of the smudge off his son's face.

Bobby added, "I left the medal inside the wreck."

"Medal?" said Hank. "What medal?"

Chapter Twenty-Three

It was early morning of Easter Sunday. Bobby rested inside the farmhouse in Pete's large bed. The others gathered either inside the first floor rooms or even braving the rain standing on the large porch. No one could leave the area due to the blocked roads covered with fallen trees.

Tawny's photographer filmed Bobby's return from the pier to the house. Tawny herself bustled around, as a reporter, asking questions of every volunteer who came ashore in the last minutes of the rescue.

The boy lay back, in good spirits, the only visible damage from his ordeal the remains of mud over his skin. The medic treated the animal bites on his legs as best he could.

Tawny photographed Bobby talking to Melissa. Her photographer pointed his video camera and she began dictating her observations.

"This is a special Easter Sunday report from the Wilderness, a large swamp outside River Sunday, Maryland. Today, we witnessed a true Easter miracle. I am here at the edge of the wetland with the child rescued from a mud-filled cave in, a horrible living grave."

She pushed the front of the camera near to the boy's face and tried to get the boy's comments in her microphone.

"How are you?'

"Better," said Bobby.

She held the mike toward the paramedic. The man in his earth-splotched River Sunday green uniform said "He's all right which is remarkable for the nightmare he's been through."

Her attention came back to Bobby. "What did you think about down in that hole?"

"My mom and dad and my grandfather. My dad saved me, and my Mom too." Bobby raised up on his stretcher and pointed to Hank who had come into the room.

Melissa, her face covered with bandages, tried to smile at Hank. "I'm proud of you," she said.

"That's my daddy," said Bobby, pointing at his father, his own clothes filthy with the tunnel dirt.

Duke, standing behind Tawny, moved to the bed and tried to get another photograph. His flash brightened the dark corners of the room.

"So it didn't get you this time," Duke said, his eyes on Hank.

Hank helped Melissa clean the dank smelling earth from Bobby's leg. "What didn't get me, Mister Duke?"

"Why, the storm, nature, the forces after you guys out there."

"No, I guess we got off this time. Old mother nature let us go."

"Sure," said Duke, "I got to thinking about that airplane. If it was old Zinnie's plane, maybe her ghost pulled strings for the boy."

Hank returned the newspaperman's stare. "Time was the problem out there. We beat it."

Mudman laughed. "You're going to disappoint the religious folks you take that attitude, Hank. People want a reason for good things."

"Why do you think this happened, Mudman?" asked Mister Duke.

He grinned, "I figure it's pretty simple. Somebody's good luck is somebody else's bad luck. Bobby gets out but Will loses his plane. We traded one for the other."

"You don't think nature is trying to get back at us for all the destruction wreaked upon it? This swamp was all dry land a few years back. These days it's so covered with water these tides can come up here and be destructive. You don't think that is nature getting even?"

"You seem to be good at analyzing that kind of thing. You write the editorial, Mister Duke," said Mudman. "I figure Bobby got himself in trouble the way a kid does."

"It's all about war anyway," Duke said. "Then again, all this happened on Easter, which is for peace."

"A guy like you can't be religious. You got to write newspaper stories," said Mudman.

Duke shook his head as Mudman walked away.

Mrs. Pond from the side of the room said, "Mister Duke, they don't get it."

Tawny spoke. "Hank, can I ask you a question?"

Hank smiled. "Sure, but Sammy and the others did most of the rescue."

She went on, "This is Hank Green, the father of the rescued child. Tell us, did you ever think the rescue hopeless?"

"I guess I had a few doubts there. My friends came through and helped me keep up my courage."

"What happens next?" asked Tawny.

"Well," said Hank, "today, Easter Sunday, is my boy's birthday."

"We have presents for him," added Melissa.

Duke said, "Sounds like a very happy day."

Father Tom entered the room. He moved through the crowd to stand next to Jimmy. Cincy, still in her raincoat, with muddy feet, followed with Mudman, still in his muddy rescue gear.

"It's a good time to give thanks," said Father Tom.

The crowd quieted as the priest asked them to bow their heads.

"Outside a great storm rages and yet inside this small room, we have witnessed the power of long ago Easter. In those days a man hung on a cross, executed, and came back to life. Here, today, on another Easter, we see the result of our prayers. The brave men and women here, working for so many hours in this storm brought life from certain death. Let us pray."

"Hank," whispered Melissa, as she bowed her head.

"Yes," he turned to her.

"I've made some pretty big mistakes about money," she said.

"You're not Judas," Hank said.

"I'm sorry. I guess I'll always think I've been taking pieces of silver. I have never stopped being your friend," she said, pressing his arm.

"Me too."

Betty put her head inside the bedroom door. "Hank, can I talk to you?"

Pete was with Betty outside the doorway. He said, "We still got one more problem here."

"What?" asked Hank, feeling his exhaustion.

Betty was close to tears. "My brother is still out there."

Pete nodded. "The last of the men got in and reported on him, Hank," he said. "Will's hanging on to a tree that came down on the tractor. Say they couldn't get to him."

"You've got to go out there, Hank," Betty said.

Sammy came over. "Will told me he was going to stay."

Pete added, "He's got nothing."

"None of the men will go," said Sammy. "The storm's got so bad and you know how they feel about the man almost killing your boy."

Sammy paused. "Folks think I'm your father, that I'm as good a fireman pulling off rescues as he was. That's the trouble. I just can't do it."

Hank was aware of how short Sammy was, that the chief was a foot shorter than Hank's father had been. He said, with a grin, "Sammy, I'm in. You drive, though. No one can handle a boat like you."

Sammy hesitated, "If you're willing to risk it, Hank, I guess I can go too."

As they got to the boat, Sammy turned and said, "I miss the days with your father. You being here, it's like he was here, too."

Hank put his hand on Sammy's shoulder. They started out from the pier. Sammy, still smiling, turned the throttle and the boat shot over the crests, pounding down with great spray, making headway. Not much was left of the Wilderness except billowing water. All the reeds had been blown down and the waves had carried them to shore. Rapid lightning strikes illuminated the water and from the glare Hank could see distant loblollies still standing out of the water, their roots stranded many feet below the surface.

Garth Brooks's thunder song came to mind, tolling.

In a sweep of Hank's flashlight, they spotted Will. With his shirt ripped and trousers ragged, his fingers grasped loblolly pine branches. The marsh water spray washed at the blood coming from cuts on his arms and legs. In his desperation, Will had tied himself by the waist to the pine trunk and he held on in such a way so that he was almost spread-eagled. He was safe but only as long as the timbers remained upright and the tide did not get any higher. Waves washed over him and Hank did not see him move as the water receded. He appeared only a dripping human form, water pouring off his immobile body like a sodden statue.

Sammy called out, "Will!" his voice as loud as he could make it in the wail of the wind. Hank joined in, both calling at the same time trying to alert Will, but each time he did not move and no sound came forth from Will's mouth.

Lightning flashed and lit up Will stretched across the wooden beams, his arms out, his face slumped. Hank thought of the Easter cross, of Christ giving his life for mankind, and of the irony of this man being symbolic of grace. He realized Christ died with criminals, those other wretches strung up like Jesus, dying in horrible pain. At the same time, he thought Will represented none of them, neither a god nor a monster, simply a selfish human fool like the rest of us.

The boat got closer. Hank, reaching out, was able to tie a line around a strong branch. Will was several feet above them. Sammy tried to stay away so the boat hull did not splinter against the tree or tractor. One good hit and the side of the boat might be crushed.

"How are we going to get him down?" shouted Sammy.

"I'll have to climb up. I'm tying a lifeline around my waist," said

Hank. He fixed the line to the central seat of the boat.

"Get ready to grab a branch," said Sammy as he brought the boat up into the wind and let it fall back. "When we get a little closer, you jump."

The boat approached again. "Jump off," yelled Sammy.

Hank reached out and wrapped his arms and legs around the pine. The rough bark tore into his skin. He began to climb and soon was several feet above the water.

Above him, he could touch Will's foot. On this foot Will still wore one of his alligator leather shoes. Hank reached Will's waist. The man's eyes were closed.

"Will," he called. The man did not answer. Hank slapped Will's face hard, trying to wake him up.

Will's eyes opened.

"You've got to come down with me," yelled Hank.

Will said, his voice very weak, "Hank, I thought I was gone for sure. Got cut up pretty bad on the tree branches."

"Come on, help me get you down."

Will shook his left arm loose from the rope attached to the trunk. He reached over and untied the fastening on his right arm.

"Try to get a good grip on me with both arms," said Hank. "I'll untie your feet."

Hank worked fast. Below, the boat lifted in another wave. Sammy called up, "Hang on, we're going to hit hard."

The boat hull crashed. Below, Sammy was thrown to his knees but managed to get back to the tiller. The engine still ran.

"No damage," called Sammy. "Hurry."

"Bring the boat back, Sammy," Hank called.

As the boat came under the tree, Hank jumped and as he did, he called to Will to do the same. Hank landed in the boat and turned to grab Will. He and Sammy managed to pull Will in and as they got aboard, another wave took the pine tree into the swamp water and washed it out of sight.

"Are you all right, Will?" asked Hank, as the man lay flat in the bilge of the boat. Sammy cut the boat hard toward the pier.

"I'm OK," mumbled Will. His eyes closed.

Hank put a piece of tarpaulin over the man to try to keep him warm.

"You got a call." Sammy handed Hank his handheld. The radio sputtered.

"Hank." It was Betty.

"We got Will. He's safe."

"Thank God."

In a few minutes, with the wind behind them, they reached the pier. Betty stood with several firemen and a stretcher. Hank helped Will climb over the side of the boat into the hands of the waiting rescue team.

Will opened his eyes.

Betty said, "You're going to be all right, Will."

Hank added, "We got Bobby, too,"

Water streamed from Will's tangled hair. "Yes," he said, "I guess you think I'm a pretty bad school teacher, don't you?"

"People do what they do."

"The airplane is gone," said Will.

"It went deep into the muck."

Hank remembered the cockpit latch cover. He reached into his pocket and felt the corroded piece of metal. He pulled it out into the light, the rain pelting it. Will was on the stretcher and the men prepared to carry him out of the rain.

"Here," said Hank, handing him the cover plate.

"What is it?" asked Will, taking it in his torn hand.

"It's part of the airplane. I got it when I was next to the wreck."

Will tightened his fist on the piece of metal and tried to wipe it dry on his wet shirt. A red tint of the original paint showed through the corrosion. Will, in great pain, pulled it toward his face, his eyes roving over it for any sign of identification. He said, without moving his head, "Thanks." He closed his eyes.

Betty reached down in the boat "Wait a minute - did you know you have another passenger?"

Hank shook his head. "No."

She helped Cochise scamper over the gunwale and off into the field.

"We ought to find some way to thank that little fellow," said Hank.

"Pete will get him some yellow water lilies to eat," said Betty.

As she walked alongside her brother's stretcher, Will turned his head toward her. "I tried to benefit our family."

"You tried for you," said Betty.

"Might be a way to go after that wreck still," said Will.

Hank stood on the pier watching Will and his sister go toward Pete's house. Betty glanced back at Hank once and her lips moved with a message of gratitude.

Mudman came out of the house with Cincy beside him.

Hank turned to his friend. "You saved me again."

"We kept a little boy alive," said Mudman, his arm held in a sling around his neck.

"Your arm broke?" asked Hank.

"Bad sprain. After the storm is over, you come out for a drink with Cincy and me."

Hank looked at Cincy and said, "Don't let him go back to Florida."

Cincy grinned and the two of them climbed on Mudman's Harley, with Cincy driving. She hitched up her raincoat and turned the key. The big engine rumbled against the sound of the wild wind and rain. Her left bare foot shifted the gear and she let out the clutch.

Pete and Hank watched them leave. The storm winds howled but the motorcycle roared defiance and splashed away.

Pete asked, "You think Will might go back out there for that plane someday?"

"He might be crazy enough," said Hank. "He needs proof for the courts."

"You think that was Zinnie's plane?" asked Pete.

Hank nodded. "She for sure got buried in the Wilderness like she wanted," he said, brushing away the last droplets of the storm from his face."

"I understand one thing." Hank said. "Jimmy's no fool. Jimmy won't let him dig unless he and his tribe get some of the profits out of those houses Will wants to build."

"Yessir, she gave the land right back to the old Native Americans her family took the land from," said Pete, moving by the crowd on his porch and opening his door.

"The Nanticokes maybe get born again," said Hank as he climbed up the porch steps to Pete's home.

"Justice," said Pete, holding his screen door for Hank.

Melissa met Hank at the door.

He asked her, "How's Bobby?"

"Come here," she said, smiling through the bandages on her face. "I want to show you something."

She opened the door to Pete's bedroom. On the large bed were the three children, asleep. Bobby was in the center, his head in a large pillow, wearing an overlarge set of Pete's pajamas. Cathy lay across the bed at Bobby's feet, still wearing the large slicker. Richard curled up against one of the bottom bedposts, his head resting in his hands.

Hank tiptoed forward, trying not to make a noise. He bent over and kissed Bobby lightly on his forehead.

Chapter Twenty-Four

"You cut your best daffodils," said Bobby, waking up in his room at Melissa's mansion. The storm had passed toward the north.

"I know you like them," said Hank. "I'm afraid most of them blew away at our store."

Bobby lay on pillows, his bed covered with wrapping paper, twisted from Bobby's opened gifts.

Melissa, a small bandage on her right cheek, stood up from her chair in the corner. "You'll want some time with Bobby alone."

"A few minutes, Mom," said Bobby.

As she started out the door, he called after her, "Mom."

She turned.

"Thanks for coming after me," he said.

She smiled at Hank and went into the hall, closing the door behind her.

"You all right?" asked Hank.

Bobby nodded yes. His eyes searched Hank's face.

"Why did you ever enter the mud cave?" began Hank. "You're too smart, Bobby."

"I wanted to bury the medal."

"What?"

"The medal I found in the letter."

"Something fell out," remembered Hank, his face blank. "I never knew your grandfather kept any medals."

"His Knight's Cross, Daddy."

Hank pulled up a chair and sat down beside his son's bed. "What is all this about? You ran out of the store. Never seen you so mad."

Bobby nodded.

"Do you want to tell me about your grandfather's letter?"

Bobby stared at him.

"What is a Knight's Cross?" asked Hank.

"Daddy, when I first read through, I didn't know what to think. Grandfather made a confession, like he told me this sin of his. He said he kept the medal but he didn't know why. Brave men got medals but he received it for being a German soldier."

Hank stared at his son. "A German soldier? I don't understand. We thought he was hiding his Jewish religion. In those days no one fought as a Jew and a German soldier at the same time."

Bobby clenched his hands. "I got so mad. I started thinking of him as a man with a whip in his hand. He wrote that when people called him a Jew in River Sunday, they reminded him of the evil committed by his native country in the war."

Hank shook his head. "Displaced people from Europe sometimes appeared to people as Jews. He didn't talk about Jews."

"You remember Mrs. Steers. Turns out she had German connections to get him false papers. Those documents in the desk are all fake. His real name was Heinrich Grien. He wasn't a Jew."

Hank stood up and walked back and forth in the small room. "Is this really true, son?"

Bobby nodded. "After reading the letter, I tried to figure out whether I loved him or hated him."

"Why didn't my father tell me all this?" asked Hank. "I thought the letter disappointed you about your boat, about not getting any money. You were so angry."

Bobby answered him. "No. Nothing about a boat. He wrote he wanted to tell me all this because I was young and not in any war, not a soldier. He said the guilty are best judged by the innocent, not by other guilty ones. I was supposed to be what Jesus spoke when he told about the pure of heart."

"I never guessed all this," said Hank. "I mean, I thought maybe a guerilla fighter or something, but not a real soldier. He didn't like war. He didn't like when I went to Vietnam."

Bobby went on, "He said maybe I would understand how he made so many mistakes, did so much damage, and then I wouldn't do the same myself. He said if he told you, you might think like a soldier and not understand his sorrow."

"I wouldn't think killing Jews was right," said Hank. "I understand why he fought for his country, though."

Bobby said, "He said he wanted to be forgiven, or at least understood, by someone not a warrior. In his letter, Daddy, Grandfather wrote he pleased his father by volunteering to join the U-Boat service."

"U-Boats?" asked Hank.

"Yes. He was a captain. Grandfather said he arrived on the American coastal patrol in the spring of 1944. The United States destroyers and aircraft attacked constantly. The depth charges terrified his crew."

Hank observed, "That explains his fear of closed places. Those subs must have been hell when the depth charges came down on them."

Bobby continued, "He wrote on Easter Sunday they surfaced to fix a problem with the dive planes. A huge storm had arrived and the boat rocked hard. He was manning the conning tower watch when the lookouts sighted a lone American warplane.

"He knew the aircraft would spot his boat soon and notify the enemy patrols. His men worked hard to get the repairs finished before a destroyer or subchaser arrived.

"The plane made a lower pass over the submarine. When the pilot opened his cockpit to get a better view, Grandfather aimed his rifle. He thought he hit him because the pilot closed the cockpit. The plane wobbled in flight and headed toward land, to the west."

Bobby paused, "He wrote that he found out later the fighter had the same number as Zinnie's plane."

"What a strange story, those two people ending up fighting each other," said Hank.

The boy continued, "All his men went below and the boat started to dive. He was the last man on the tower. A destroyer attacked. He wrote the storm was so bad the ship came on them without being seen in the high waves.

"The destroyer cut right through the metal of the submarine hull, the sub bending in half. Both ships blew up. With the impact he felt himself being thrown in the air and twisted around, almost flying, until he hit the water surface about fifty feet away. Dead bodies were floating around him.

"The current brought him toward shore. The destroyer bow section moved ahead of him. It crunched, upside down, into the sand beach a hundred yards from him."

"The wreck remained on that beach for years," said Hank.

"He dressed in the clothes of an American sailor. When the beach patrol arrived, he hid among the dunes. He ran inland, far away from the beach. In the sailor's clothes he passed as American when he met people on the road."

Hank said, "He must have been in pretty bad shape."

"He was. He knew about a German agent and went to her house. She helped him hide."

"That must have been Missus Steers. She was the only one suspected by the authorities in the area. Nothing was ever proved."

Bobby nodded. "He became her gardener during the rest of the war."

Hank said, "People in River Sunday claimed U-boats anchored near her house to pick up gold from Nazi sympathizers before the war started. Grandfather would never say anything bad about her."

Bobby asked, "Should I have left the medal in the swamp?"

"You did the right thing. The medal rests in the swamp mud with Zinnie's ring. If anyone ever finds the plane, the town will have a mystery about all of this."

"Jimmy said the Native American heroes were buried there. I figured the mound a good place. Grandfather was a hero to his own people."

"How did he get the medal?"

"He wrote he was awarded the Cross for bravery in sinking ships coming into England. He said he got it even though he was not a member of the Nazi Party."

Bobby stared at his father. "What will you do, Daddy? You must think about Grandfather, too."

"I will try to understand him," Hank said. "You know, Bobby, he could have died never having told us anything. I think this letter was an act of love."

"A weird one."

"I agree," said Hank.

"I did decide to keep on loving him," said Bobby.

"I guess I will, too," said Hank. He went on, "While you were talking, I started to think we might not even be citizens."

Bobby frowned.

Hank grinned. "Then I remembered the law. We're citizens because we were born here. So, you left the medal and letter in the plane?"

"I tore little pieces, balled them up, and fed them to the muskrats. Kept them busy too. I listened to them chomping away."

Hank began to laugh.

Bobby, grinning, began to laugh, too.

Melissa knocked and opened the door slightly. "What are you guys laughing about?"

Bobby spoke quickly, "Some secrets a father and son got, Mom. Come on in. We're all done."

"Maybe we ought to try to help the white muskrat after the water goes down. I mean, get him a new home," suggested Melissa.

Betty followed her into the room.

Hank said, "The mound will come back up after the water recedes." He smiled at Melissa saying something positive about animals.

"The white one only," she added.

"I'm going to rename him Sachem," said Bobby.

"Is Will all right?" asked Hank.

"He's fine. He's down the hall in bed figuring out how to dredge out the P47," said Betty.

Bobby asked, "Where're Cathy and Richard?"

"They will be here later to visit you."

Later Betty and Hank walked down the littered street in River Sunday. They approached the colonial courthouse still untouched and serene among the nearby churches for which River Sunday owed its name.

On the street, families passed them, returning from Easter services.

Stevie Nicks and her Fleetwood Mac song "Landslide" eased through his mind. He slowed his pace to keep time.

To the left of the courthouse in a boxwood garden stood the Confederate memorial, forever looming over the life of River Sunday, its bronze battle flag tarnished by a thousand rains.

With the rhythm of the song still in his ears, Hank glanced to the right of the Courthouse door where a statue stood of Frederick Douglas the famous Northern leader, born into slavery near on a plantation near River Sunday. A rough marble stone with a brass plaque about Zinnie Allingham rested on the ground to the right of the Douglas monument. It was heavily overgrown.

Hank asked Betty to wait as he cleared some of the long grass. He pulled back a section of the surrounding boxwood to make sure a bit of afternoon sunlight shimmered on the wet brass.

"I never read these words," he said.

Melusina Allingham
Easter, 1944
"She used her light to free others from earth's darkness"

Hank touched the stone with respect.

"I've got to get my tools and come over here and clip back more branches," he said to Betty as she crouched beside him. "You can't even see the inscription and that's a shame for a heroine."

He said, "Strange how that black Nazi cross ended up buried in the Wilderness with her ivory crucifix."

"Evil and good," she said.

"Wonder which one will survive the mud in the future?" he said, looking into the eyes of his old friend.

She nodded and kissed him softly on his mouth.

"What was that for?" he smiled.

"I should have done that a long time ago," she said.

"Yeah, maybe we both should have," he said, reaching his hand up to caress her cheek.

"From now on, I'm going to help you plant your daffodils, Greenie."

Acknowledgements

Acknowledgements: The author wishes to thank C. Michael Curtis of the Atlantic Monthly for his kindness and encouragement in the writing of Easter Sunday. Also thanks are due in remembrance of my former mentor, Elliott Coleman, of Johns Hopkins University. Gratitude is extended to the dedicated, professional and extremely knowledgeable staff of the United States Department of the Interior, Fish and Wildlife Service, Blackwater National Wildlife Refuge in Cambridge, Maryland, for touring the author through the swamp and teaching him much good lore about muskrats. The author hopes all the wetlands in the country have people of this quality taking care of them.

Songs referenced in the book are "Green Green Grass of Home" by Johnny Darrell, Music and Lyrics by Curly Putman and Sheb Worley, 1965, "Landslide" by Fleetwood Mac, music and lyrics by Stevie Nicks, 1975, "Blowin' in the Wind," Bob Dylan, 1962, "Wind Beneath My Wings, Jeff Silban and Larry Henley, 1982, "The Thunder Rolls," Garth Brooks and Pat Alger, 1991.

Finally thanks are given to the research staff of the Boston Athenaeum for its hard work in sourcing books for research on various aspects of this story. Last but not least thanks to my fiction workshop friends for their suggestions on some of the chapters and to my family for their patience.

About the Author

Thomas Hollyday brings to life strong Chesapeake characters showcased in their stunning, unique Eastern seaboard landscapes. Reviewers praise his rich sense of place and his respect for the great machines that made our era possible. His stories resonate with a deep awareness of history and legend. The humor in life shines through as Tom draws on a comedic sense honed sharp from an accomplished cartooning background. His characters have the depth and insight learned from a business life in international trade and as president of a manufacturing company building animal watering systems.

In his River Sunday Romance Mysteries series, Tom honors the battles for love of land that have recurred over and over in the Chesapeake Bay. Past victories and defeats created mists of legend and history which shroud the present landscapes. Throughout Tom's stories, he incorporates both the machines that have left lasting imprints and the wildlife that enriches the captivating natural landscape. His modern and timely novels feature memorable characters from the small town of River Sunday, Maryland, and reveal their compelling stories as they search for answers to achieving love, unveiling mystery, and vanquishing evil.

Tom grew up in the Chesapeake Bay, and his love for his native land shines through in every word.

Part of the proceeds from the sale of Thomas Hollyday fiction and non-fiction goes to support drinking water resources for wildlife.

Check out other novels in the River Sunday Romance Mystery Series:

Slave Graves
Magnolia Gods
Gold
Powerboat Racer
Terror Flower
China Jewel
Easter Sunday

These books can be found in paperback from Amazon and Barnes and Noble and Ebook format from most major online retailers including Amazon, iTunes, Kobo, Smashwords and Nook. Select bookstores carry these books in print.

For more information, and to talk with Tom, visit:

To see his latest blogs:
https://achesapeakewriterblog.wordpress.com/

To list for his free newsletter: http://solarsippers.com

To see reviews of his books on Facebook:
https://www.facebook.com/RiverSundayRomanceMysteries

To tweet: Twitter: @tomholly

Made in the USA
Monee, IL
07 July 2026